DANGEROUS DESIRE

A HOLIDAY ROMANCE

MICHELLE LOVE

HOT AND STEAMY ROMANCE

CONTENTS

1. Chapter One   1
2. Chapter Two   6
3. Chapter Three   11
4. Chapter Four   16
5. Chapter Five   20
6. Chapter Six   27
7. Chapter Seven   33
8. Chapter Eight   42
9. Chapter Nine   47
10. Chapter Ten   50
11. Chapter Eleven   55
12. Chapter Twelve   65
13. Chapter Thirteen   72
14. Chapter Fourteen   79
15. Chapter Fifteen   87
16. Chapter Sixteen   95
17. Chapter Seventeen   101
18. Chapter Eighteen   106
19. Chapter Nineteen   112
20. Chapter Twenty   117
21. Chapter Twenty-One   121
22. Chapter Twenty-Two   125
23. Chapter Twenty-Three   133
24. Chapter Twenty-Four   138
25. Chapter Twenty-Five   148
26. Chapter Twenty-Six   152
27. Chapter Twenty-Seven   156
28. Chapter Twenty-Eight   161
29. Chapter Twenty-Nine   168
30. Chapter Thirty   175
31. Chapter Thirty-One   180
32. Chapter Thirty-Two   185

33. Chapter Thirty-Three   188
34. Chapter Thirty-Four   191

About the Author   195

Made in "The United States" by:

Michelle Love

© Copyright 2020

ISBN: 978-1-64808-715-8

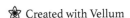 Created with Vellum

BLURB

Satchel

From the first moment, Winter Mai had me hooked.
Her beauty, her will to survive...
But she hates me—and with good reason.
My best friend, my brother, murdered her sister and almost killed
Winter, too.
She doesn't know about the sleepless nights I spent silently begging
her to live...
And now, all these years later, she's right in front of me, and in the
arms of a man I know to be a violent and dangerous criminal.
I won't let anything hurt her. I owe her...
...and I'm desperately—achingly—in love with her.
Will she ever forgive me?
Her face and her body haunt my dreams, and I won't be happy until
Winter is my arms, my life, and my bed...

Winter

How did I get myself into this?

Raziel Ganz is the opposite of what I was looking for and now I
know... he's a dangerous man and he won't let me go.

But my heart lies elsewhere, with a man whom I've hated from afar
for so long that when I actually meet him in person, I despise the way
my body reacts to him...
Satchel Rose.

The best friend of the man who murdered my sister. The man who testified for her killer.
But...
The electricity between us is undeniable—all-consuming—and I hate myself for wanting his hands on my body...
...but, God help me, it's all I can think about...

Young Winter Mai is rebuilding her life after a tragedy tore her sister away forever. Living a solitary life on a houseboat, she finds herself drawn into the world of a billionaire businessman who moors his luxury yacht next to her home.
Raziel Ganz knows what he wants, and when he sees the beautiful Winter, he knows he wants to possess her, and he is not a man to be denied. When he sets out to seduce her, Winter succumbs to his charms, but she soon realizes he is not who he says he is.
After meeting Satchel Rose, a local property magnate whom Ganz is trying to schmooze, Winter realizes that love at first sight does exist when the connection between them crackles and fizzles with undeniable heat. But Satchel has history with Winter's family and with the tragedy that took her sister...
Mired in a relationship she doesn't want, Winter soon realizes that Raziel isn't a man to defy—*no one* leaves him...
At turns, tumultuous, romantic, and full of danger, Satchel and Winter's love flourishes before an unexpected pregnancy complicates matters, and Raziel Ganz attempts to destroy their passion. Will Winter and Satchel get their happy ever after?

CHAPTER ONE

*P*ortland Harbor, Oregon

AS USUAL, it was the fireworks that triggered her. The sound of the *pop-pop-pop-pop-pop* in the night sky above the harbor was endless, and although Winter tried all the techniques the counselor had taught her, she still ended up trembling underneath the bunk in her bedroom.

She squeezed her eyes shut and tried to visualize her happy place, playing with her childhood dog, Crunchy, in the wheat fields of her youth in Kokomo, Indiana. Those few years when her father was stationed at that military base were the happiest of Winter's life.

Pop-pop-pop-pop-pop. It's just fireworks, that is all it is...

Blood. Screaming. Terror. An ordinary Saturday afternoon shopping with her sister at the mall...

Pop-pop-pop-pop-pop.

She hears a strange keening sound, like a wounded animal, except the sound is coming from *her,* and she stuffs her hands into her own mouth to stop herself. Anyone close by would wonder why she was screaming, and out here on her tiny houseboat in Portland Harbor, a million miles away from where it had happened, they might come to help her.

The last thing she needed now were strangers on her boat, in her home. Her skin itched at the thought of it.

Finally, just after one a.m. the fireworks ended, and Winter crawled out panting from under the bunk. She sat with her knees drawn up to her chest and took several deep breaths. Her chest felt fluttery, her psyche fragile, and she let a few hot tears fall down her cheeks before she rebuked herself.

You're twenty-seven years old, Winter Mai. You're an adult. Fireworks are just that. Fireworks.

She scrambled to her feet—too quickly—and grabbed the edge of the bunk as she swayed, dizzy. Her back was aching from being scrunched up beneath the bunk, and she stretched it out with a couple of yoga moves, pretending to herself that she was relaxing.

In reality, her ears were tuned, ready for more. Fear was turning into anger. Who the hell was letting off fireworks? It was early November; Thanksgiving still three weeks away. It wasn't an election year nor had any other big event occurred.

Just some assholes celebrating a goddamned birthday or something, and fuck everyone else's peace, Winter thought angrily now. That irritation propelled her out onto her deck to seek out the perpetrator despite her frazzled nerves.

The culprit wasn't difficult to spot. The vast yacht that was moored in the harbor had arrived two days ago and was now jam-packed with people. A party. A thick pall of smoke hung about it, and Winter could still see small fireworks being set off from it. *Assholes.*

To make herself feel better, she gave it the finger with both hands and stomped back inside.

Winter shut her door and sunk down into her ancient but comfortable sofa, glancing at the clock. She had a nine o'clock appointment in the morning to give a piano lesson to one of her students, so sleep was definitely the best idea now... except she knew it wouldn't come. Truthfully, her constant nightmares prevented her from getting any solid sleep nowadays, and it was only when she took a sleeping pill that she got any rest at all.

But they made her feel so crappy the next day... *no*. She got up and went to take a shower. Even in the cold of an Oregon winter, she was sweating and clammy from the terror of the fireworks. She stripped off and studied herself in the floor-length mirror. She could do with gaining a couple of pounds; her slight frame the result from a lack of appetite and not being able to afford much food. All her money, all the awarded compensation from the... 'thing'... had gone into buying this houseboat; now she had to live paycheck-to-paycheck from the small amount of money she earned as a freelance piano tutor.

That didn't matter, she thought now. *I don't need money. I just want peace...* and for most of the time, that's what this little haven in Portland gave her. She didn't see many people—didn't *want* to see anyone —except for the few students she had, and she was very lucky to have them.

Winding her long dark hair up into a bun, Winter stepped into the shower. The daughter of a Chinese-American father and a Dutch mother, she was the youngest of three sisters. Her two older siblings, Summer and Autumn, were older by two and four years respectively, the latter a famed celebrity chef now back in New York. Summer had been with Winter when the shooting happened.

Winter survived, although badly injured. *Summer...*

Summer didn't make it.

Winter stood under the water until it turned cold, but she still felt like her skin was on fire. She pressed her hands to the scars across her chest and stomach. The bullets had missed her major organs and arteries, unbelievably so, considering she had been shot six times, but Summer hadn't been so lucky.

Stop it. Winter shook herself, cranking off the shower faucet and stepping, shivering now, out of the shower. She dried herself quickly and dressed in jeans and a sweater, tugging on thick socks and her sneakers.

After busying herself with making a cup of tea, Winter stepped out onto her houseboat deck. It was bitingly cold, but that's what she wanted—the cool air on her skin. She sat down on the small love seat and sipped her fragrant tea. While watching the fete slowly break up and partygoers boisterously leaving the yacht, she could see them thanking a tall man, dark and exquisitely dressed in a dark grey suit and a blue shirt. She guessed him to be in his forties, carrying an athletic build with strong legs and broad shoulders. His hair was cut short, and his face was handsome, as chiseled as a Roman God. He was clearly the owner of the yacht, and Winter wondered who he was.

Wondering the name of the man I should hate for putting me through this night. She knew she was scowling, but she didn't care; she even hoped he would see her and realize he had upset her. Winter hoped some of the other people who lived here would be out of their homes as well, giving him hell for keeping them awake.

But she guessed that none of them likely react to fireworks the way she does. She sighed. She hated this time of year; so many noisy holidays that could provoke more nights like this: Thanksgiving, Christmas, New Year. Along with July 4th, they were her least favorite days of the year, but at least she could expect them—prepare. Noise cancelling headphones and Pearl Jam at full blast. When she could afford it, she would drive to a motel out in the middle of nowhere on July 4th just to avoid all the fireworks and celebrations.

But when they were unexpected, like tonight, she had no time to prepare. *Fuck...* Winter knew she would be upset for days now, her equilibrium rocked. She sighed and closed her eyes. Another sleepless night was on its way unless she gave in to that little bottle of pills on her bathroom sink.

RAZIEL GANZ SAID goodbye to the last of his guests and made his way back up to the now-darkened party deck. For the last hour or so, he'd been waiting to be alone, so he could study the young woman sitting out on the deck of the small houseboat moored next to his yacht. He had seen her storm out and make the crude gesture towards his yacht just after the fireworks had finished, and it had amused him greatly.

Not only that, but the girl was achingly beautiful: bi-racial, he guessed; Asian; her almond eyes; the olive skin; the dark hair tumbling around her shoulders—an exquisite face even in anger.

It had been a while since Raziel Ganz had been surprised by a woman. The ladies that he attracted knew of his wealth and tried to land him as a partner, a future husband, but he wasn't interested in commitment—not with those women. Where was the challenge, the fire, the excitement?

No. He'd much rather spar with the young woman who owned that damn ramshackle houseboat. She was clearly unimpressed by wealth, and that was thrilling to him.

At forty-four, Raziel Ganz presented an aura of corporate wealth, ruthless business acumen, and dazzling good looks to the world, and he enjoyed everything that brought him. He slept around, yes, but rarely called any of the woman back—no, scratch that—he *never* called *any* woman back.

This woman, though, might prove interesting. She would certainly look good on his arm when he met Satchel Rose, his mark for this visit to Portland. Rose was notoriously private—elusive *and* reclusive—and the fact he'd agreed to a meeting with Raziel was a major victory. If Raziel wanted to move some of his shipping corporation to Portland, he would have to have Rose on side to secure the city's welcome.

And Rose would give him the air of authenticity that he needed to cover his real business...

For now though, Raziel lit a cigarette and watched the beauty on the houseboat. She seemed to sense his scrutiny and glared up in his direction. As he watched, amused, she again threw a middle finger up, got up, and stalked back into her home, slamming the door behind her.

Raz smiled. *Yes.* She would be his kind of challenge.

CHAPTER TWO

"You look like crap."

Winter half-grinned at her student and her friend. "Always such a silver-tongued devil. Thank you."

Joseph Matts, his hair coaxed up into a Mohican, shrugged. "Sorry, boo, but it's unusual for you to look bad, so it's more noticeable." He checked himself. Joseph was bipolar and sometimes spoke his mind without thinking. "Sorry. I meant that as a compliment."

Winter's smile was wide now. "I know, honey." She rubbed his back. Joe was one of the few people she could stand to be around, which was why she considered him her friend as well as a paying student.

Joe was around her age, maybe even a little older, and was a sensational musician. He was way past what Winter would consider as needing lessons, but the truth was, she knew Joe felt comfortable with her, and she helped him write songs for his two-man band. Joe's wife, Cassie, was also a friend; she and Joe so in love that it made Winter's heart ache. Cassie kept Joe steady, managing his medication and his moods with an expert touch. Winter always told her she had the looks of a cheerleader and the brain of a Nobel Prize winner.

Cassie was a sweetheart even if she did tend to 'mother' Winter a little. Winter didn't mind that so much.

Joe sat down at the piano as Winter grabbed her folder. "What were we doing last time?"

"New song. The one about darkness."

"They're *all* about darkness," Winter shot back with a laugh. "We're the cheerful twins, remember?"

"Word." Joe grinned at her. "You know, I was talking to Josh... we could always use a third member."

"Ha, thanks, but no thanks. I'm not a performer. Not anymore."

She was interrupted by a knock on the door of her houseboat. Winter and Joe frowned at each other. She never got unplanned visitors. Winter got up and went to the door. A smiling delivery man greeted her and handed her a huge hamper. "Courtesy of Mr. Ganz. An apology for the inconvenience of his party last night."

Before Winter could react, the man had gone. She staggered back inside with the heavy hamper and dumped it on her couch.

"What the hell?" Joseph was up, looking curious. Winter sighed.

"Dude in the big yacht next door trying to buy my forgiveness for keeping me awake all night. Which is why I look like crap, by the way. I can't keep this."

Joe held his hands up, grinning. "Woah, woah! Wait until you check out what's inside."

"Joe."

"I'm serious. Come on, open up."

Sighing, Winter opened up the hamper reluctantly, sincerely wanting to just reject it immediately.

"Damn." Joseph whistled, and Winter gaped at what was inside: Champagne, caviar, truffles, and a myriad of artisanal cold cuts, cheeses, and other luxury foods. Joe plucked the card from the hamper. "Read! Read!"

Winter snatched it from him, grinning. "Damn, boy, you are so nosy." She opened it and read aloud what it said. "Please accept my apologies for the disturbance last night, dear lady. I hope this goes some way to making up for it. Perhaps you would like to join me for drinks tonight? Raziel Ganz." She rolled her eyes. "*Dear lady?*"

Joe snorted. "Perhaps he and Mr. Darcy teamed up to write that card. How does he know he upset you?"

Winter grinned. "I gave him the bird. Twice. He might not have seen the first time, but he definitely saw the second time." She felt pleased that her nemesis had seen her anger. She looked down at the hamper. It had to be said, this food would be a welcome asset to her bare cupboards—she'd been living on ramen and pasta for the last week or so. Joe was watching her carefully.

"Win? There would be nothing wrong with keeping this, you know? You wouldn't owe him anything but a polite thank you."

Winter flushed. Joe was one of the few people who knew she struggled to make ends meet—he and Cassie often invited Winter over to eat with them, and Cassie always managed to send Winter home with the leftovers. Winter wished she didn't need to take their kind charity, but a girl needed to eat. She paid them back by working with Joe for his songwriting and not charging for the extra time. It made her feel as if she were giving something back at least. "It's a lot."

"Well, he kept you awake, and I know how you feel about fireworks..."

Winter nodded. "Yup." She grinned ruefully. "I have to admit, that ham looks amazing."

"It does, and you know what, that reminds me... Cassie and I would love to have you over for Thanksgiving... if you're not with your family, of course."

Winter's heart sank. "No. I won't be with them." Not for a couple of years now, and she couldn't see a time when she would be again.

Joe rubbed her shoulder. "Then it's decided."

She smiled at him. He may look like a punk rocker who didn't give a crap, but Joe really was the sweetest guy she had ever known. He felt like family to her now as did Cassie; Joe was the brother Winter had never had. "If you're sure?"

"Very. Now, should we get on?"

Winter nodded, closing the hamper and leaving the card on top. She'd decide what to do about it later. "We should. Let's get to it."

RAZIEL HAD SMILED to himself when he saw the delivery guy turn up at the girl's houseboat with the hamper. He watched as surprise registered on her lovely face, then a stiff nod. She wasn't someone who took charity, he could see that.

And now he knew her name as well. Winter Mai. His private investigator had taken less than an hour to find about her. Twenty-seven and a piano tutor. Living alone. No family in the Portland area. Survived the mall shooting massacre in Seattle a few years back, but was seriously injured.

Ah. Raz suddenly understood the reason for her anger last night. *The fireworks. Damn.* Well, at least he could apologize for that and cancel his plans for any further shows. It was the least he could do. His private investigator had turned up some photos of her, too. Christ, she was stunning. Dark brown eyes, olive skin, long dark hair with burnished mahogany highlights. A petite curvy body: soft, sensual. His gaze lingered over that exquisite face and that pink rosebud mouth—so inviting, so kissable.

Yes. She would be a challenge, but he was confident he could seduce her. *Good.* He was bored with the usual suspects when it came to his bed partners. He wondered how long she would hold out before she succumbed to his charms... it wouldn't be long.

He turned as his personal assistant, Gareth, knocked at his office door and came in. "Hey, boss."

"Gareth. What's on for today?"

"Unfortunately there's still no confirmation from the Satchel Rose camp on when he'll meet with you, but I do have intel he'll be at a function for the Portland Public Library in a couple of weeks."

Raz's eyebrows shot up. "Rose? Out in public?"

Gareth smiled. "Seems he has ties to the library—family ties, I think. Not quite sure in what manner."

"Find out, would you? And call the library. Tell them I'd like to attend."

"Sure thing."

WHEN HE WAS ALONE, Raziel's thoughts turned back to the beautiful young woman on the houseboat. He would go see her personally this afternoon to give her little room to reject him.

Winter Mai would be the perfect date for the library benefit and to meet Satchel Rose, and he, Raziel, always got what he wanted.

Always.

CHAPTER THREE

Satchel Rose sighed as someone knocked at his study door. He'd hoped not to be interrupted for the morning, so he could indulge in his favorite task: designing buildings. He'd gotten a couple of hours of drawing and planning done, but now his assistant was interrupting his flow, and he knew he wouldn't get it back again. "Come in."

Molly stuck her head around the door, an apologetic expression on her sweet face. "I'm sorry, Satch. I wouldn't interrupt, but your father called again. Wanted to get your yes or no for Thanksgiving, and he insisted I come ask you. I think he's worried you won't turn up and referee."

Satchel smiled despite himself. His father, Patrick, was a loving but weak-willed man who was terrified of his new wife, Janelle. Satchel, on the other hand, *adored* Janelle, although he jokingly called her his step-monster. The African-American college professor gave as good as she got, teasing Satchel mercilessly, and also ruling her husband's life, challenging him, egging him on, not letting him rest on his laurels in his retirement. They'd been together for twenty years but had only recently tied the knot.

Satchel smiled at Molly now. "I'll call the house, Mols. Thanks."

"No problem, boss."

Satchel called the house; both his father and Janelle refused to get cellphones, which Satchel found cute and annoying in equal measure. Janelle answered his call.

"Hey, Brat."

"Hey, Monster. I have been summoned."

Janelle laughed, her giggle mischievous. "Your dad is crapping his pants. I told him all my sisters and my mom are coming to Thanksgiving. It's not true, of course, but he's convinced he'll be outnumbered."

Satchel laughed loudly. "You really are *evil*. I love it."

"Here's your dad. Don't rat me out..." she whispered before raising her voice slightly. Satchel's dad was a little deaf. "Your son, or so he says. I think he's actually the spawn of the devil." She cackled with laughter, then her voice grew fond as she spoke to Satchel again. "Just kidding. Love you, Brat. Bye, sweetie."

"Bye, gorgeous. Love you, too." Satchel waited until his dad took the phone and said hello. "Hey, Pa, how are you doing?"

"*Women.*" Patrick said with a quiver in his voice. "There's going to be women everywhere. She has six sisters, Satch! *Six!*"

Satchel grinned to himself. "Pa, most men would be grateful to be surrounded by women."

"Six sisters, Satchel. *Six. And* the mother."

"You love Janelle's family, come on."

Patrick harrumphed. "I love them... from a distance. Just promise me you'll be there."

"I promise, Pa. Calm down."

That seemed to settle his father. "Bringing anyone? How about that Molly? She's a sweetheart; I don't know why you haven't snapped her up."

"Because, Pa, I possess something that she isn't the least bit interested in."

"What could that possibly be, son?"

Satchel grinned. "A penis, Pa. I've told you before. Molly is very happily married to a wonderful woman."

More grumbling and muttering from his father, and Satchel laughed. "Pa, look, there's no one at the moment, and I'm fine with that."

"There hasn't been for a couple of years, Satch. I'm worried."

"Pa... come on. I'm too old for you to be worrying about that." Satchel swallowed the irritation that always bubbled up when his dad fretted about his son's lack of love life. "I'm fussy, and I like my own space."

"Hermit."

"Yup, unashamedly so."

There was a short silence on the end of the line. "As long as you're not still blaming yourself for... you know."

Satchel's chest felt tight. "No, Pa." A lie—and they both knew it. "Look, I have to go. I'll be at Thanksgiving, I promise."

"Good. Love you, son."

"Love you, too, Pa."

He hung up and rubbed his face as he headed to the small executive bathroom next to his office. Satchel worked from home as much as possible, but even his home was set out like an office, with Molly having her own private space in which to work. She was about the only person he could stand to be around for long periods, but even then, sometimes he felt the overwhelming need to be alone. Luckily, Molly seemed to sense when he was going through one of his hermit phases and would leave him alone as much as she could, running interference on people who wanted more time than Satchel was willing to give.

Satchel splashed water on his face and studied his reflection. At almost forty, he knew he had aged into a handsome man, but his looks were a hindrance as far as Satchel was concerned. Dark hair, swarthy skin from his late Italian mother, and bright green eyes were like catnip to both women and men. When he had been younger, he had been a beautiful boy and had made the most of it: sleeping around, enjoying life. Being sociable. When had that changed?

You know when, he told himself. He closed his eyes, scrunching them up. God, when he would he just get over it? *It wasn't your fault*

Callan Flint went crazy with that gun. It wasn't your responsibility to 'save' him.

So why did he feel like it was? Ever since the St Anne's Mall massacre, Satchel had felt himself withdrawing from public life. Callan had been his best friend, and he hadn't noticed how bad things had gotten.

No one had, but Satchel was the person closest to Callan, and even he hadn't seen it. Twenty-seven people dead. Fifty three injured. Satchel had paid for every funeral and all the medical expenses and had to be stopped from giving away all of his money to the survivors. Callan's parents had stepped in then. "Satchel, this isn't your fault. We need to do something, too—make reparations."

And so, the Flint family had paid out compensation to the victims. It wasn't like they couldn't afford it—both the Rose and Flint families were billionaires several times over. But for Satchel, it didn't feel as he'd done enough. He became increasingly despondent and only found peace when he was alone.

He pushed those thoughts aside for now, knowing they would return as they always did to routinely haunt his days. To distract himself, he powered on the television and flicked through the channels. He stopped when he came to a food and cooking channel, his attention caught by the woman presenting. Autumn Mai. He knew that name all too well. The Mai family. Three sisters, Autumn, Summer, and Winter. Autumn was the only one of them left physically unscathed by the shooting. Summer had been killed by a single bullet to her throat. Winter, the youngest, had been the worst of the injured, shot six times in the chest and stomach at point-blank range and not expected to live.

Satchel, unbeknownst to everyone, had often sat by the young woman's bed late at night, after visiting hours. It was time his money could buy. He didn't know her at all and hadn't spoken to her family, but there was something so vulnerable about her. Christ, she was just a kid.

Then, without warning, one day her family secretly transferred her to a different hospital, and he lost track of her. It felt like a death.

He'd been channeling all his guilt into this one victim, and when she was removed from his life, his guilt had nowhere to go but internally.

He watched her older sister now, Autumn. A celebrity chef even before the shooting, she was confident and affable on screen and obviously loved her chosen profession. A stunningly beautiful woman, her Asian parentage obvious in her features and her dark hair piled up on her head as she moved gracefully around the set.

Satchel sighed. Maybe he could get past the guilt if he found out where Autumn's sister had gone. If he could see her, apologize to her in person...

But that would be an incredible invasion of privacy and selfish of him, too. No, he had to face his demons on his own.

He just didn't know where the hell to start.

CHAPTER FOUR

*S*he was screaming now, begging Summer to breathe... Her sister's eyes were open, staring, so she must be okay, right? "That's it, Sum, look at me. Breathe... breathe..."

But Summer wouldn't take a breath—not ever again. The blood on her neck, the hole in her throat...

Winter screamed and screamed, before hearing the gun click right behind her. She whirled around to face her sister's killer, and he pressed the gun against her body and shot her, the bullets slamming into her belly...

She went down, and he stood over her, firing again and again and again...

"No!" Winter sat up in her bunk, breathing heavily, dragging precious oxygen into her lungs. She spent a few moments catching her breath, calming herself.

Slowly, the sound of music seeped into her brain, the irritating thumpa-thumpa-thumpa of a heavy dance beat.

"You have got to be fucking kidding me," she growled and got up, pushing back the bedroom curtain.

That asshole was having *another* party. "Nope. No fucking way."

Winter, incensed, and riding on adrenaline from her nightmare, tugged on her jeans and an old T-shirt and stomped up on deck. In her bare feet, she stalked along the jetty and pushed past the bodyguard without speaking to him. She was surprised that he didn't make any attempt to stop her, and a moment later, she heard him speaking into his walkie-talkie. "She's on her way up, boss."

What the hell? But Winter was too riled up to stop now. She had no idea where she was going, but eventually she found herself on the main deck. To her surprise, there was no crowd of people and she stopped, frowning. She hadn't imagined it; she'd seen them on the deck, crowding around a few moments earlier.

"Miss Mai."

She whirled around to see him, Raziel Ganz, smiling at her. "If you're wondering where everyone went... they went back to their rooms. My staff." He looked around and spoke aloud to some unknown person. "Cut the music, would you?"

The music stopped, the bright lights dimmed, and just a string of small white lights lit the deck. Winter was confused. "You... what the hell is going on here?"

Gan smiled. "You didn't reply to my invitation, so I thought I'd try a more imaginative approach." He titled his head to the side. "And you're beautiful when you're angry."

Hell, no. "So, this was a trick?"

"A plot, yes."

"It's creepy," she said, no humor in his tone. "And I don't appreciate it."

Raziel shrugged. "Then I misread the situation and I apologize. But you're here now... Can I at least apologize for last night in person?"

Winter wasn't in any mood for a rich man's games. "You did that with the hamper. Which I can't accept, obviously."

"And yet you didn't send it back. Curious."

Winter flushed. *Asshole.* "Not yet, but I assure you, Mr...? I'm sorry, I don't remember your name." A cheap shot but she enjoyed it.

"Call me Raz. You can assure me of what?"

"The 'gift,' 'apology,' whatever you want to call it... will be returned untouched. I do not accept your apology. I just want you to be considerate of the people who live here on the harbor."

Raziel Ganz held up his hands. "You're completely right, of course."

That stopped her. "What?"

Raz sat down at one of the tables and nodded to the chair opposite for her to sit. "You're right. It was selfish and inconsiderate of me to throw a party without at least considering the inhabitants here. You must think me a rich, spoiled man."

Winter was a little disarmed by that, and she slowly took the seat, narrowing her eyes at him. "Aren't you?"

"I am, I admit. I am. But I'm also just a man. I make mistakes. I'm sorry, Winter."

He seemed genuine and Winter felt her anger dissipate. "So, this whole ruse was in aid of what?"

Raziel grinned and his whole face lit up. There was no denying he was a spectacularly handsome man. "A little payback. For the three bird-flipping incidents."

Winter smirked then. "You deserved them."

"I did. And I wanted to meet you."

Winter half-smiled. "You could have just come and said hello. I'm right there."

She pointed down at her home, which, she had to admit, looked a wreck next to this behemoth of a boat. "But why would you want to meet *me*? Of all people?"

Raziel smiled. "Because you're different. You don't kiss ass. You don't care about all this." He waved his hand around casually.

"You get all that from a couple of rude gestures?" Winter was bemused but Raziel nodded.

"I do. Plus... I will be upfront; I asked around about you. People here really like you, Winter."

She flushed at the compliment, a warm feeling blooming in her chest. She was touched, but she didn't want to show it to this man.

This man, who she hated to admit, was surprising her. She liked that he didn't pretend that he wasn't absurdly privileged, but also that he knew there was more to life, to a person, than wealth. "Who *are* you, Mr. Ganz?"

He chuckled. "It's Raz, please, and my business is shipping, but I'm hoping to move into property. Portland is one of the most up-and-coming cities in the word right now. I want in."

"I see." She didn't know what else to say to that. What did she, a piano tutor, know about shipping?

"Winter... have dinner with me tomorrow night. No pressure, just dinner."

She gave a confused chuckle. "Why?"

"Because I like you, and I want to get to know you."

She studied him for a long time. "I won't be one of your conquests, Raziel."

"Like I said, just dinner. No expectation except for your company. That's all I ask."

Winter opened her mouth to refuse him—and instead found herself saying yes.

RAZIEL WATCHED her walk back to her houseboat, pleased when she turned to look back at him. He waved, and she raised an unsure hand in reply. Raziel smiled, seeing her disappear back into that pathetic ramshackle place of hers.

Oh, you will *be one of my conquests, Winter Mai. I'll give you a life far away from that floating dump, and you'll wonder why you ever went up against me.*

I always get what I want, Winter. And I want you...

CHAPTER FIVE

Winter had no idea what would be expected of her, dress wise, for dinner with Raziel Ganz, but then again, it had been so long since she'd been out.

"It's just freaking dinner," she told herself angrily and pulled out a dark green dress from the depths of her closet. She hadn't worn this since before the shooting, remembering that night. It had been one of Autumn's book launches in Manhattan; the three sisters had giggled their way through the party, garnering disapproving looks from Helga, the aunt who had raised them after their parents died. Each in turn, the sisters teased their aunt as she got increasingly starstruck by the celebrities turning up for the launch.

"Is that George Clooney?" Helga had asked in an urgent whisper, and her nieces enjoyed teasing her that she was in love with the movie star.

Winter smiled now, but the familiar ache returned to her chest. Helga and Autumn were still in Manhattan, still trying to reach out to her. Only today, Autumn had left her a message on her voicemail. *Please, Winnie... come home. For Thanksgiving. It's time.*

Winter had deleted it before it could make her cry. *Please,* she thought, *don't make this harder than it already is.* The sound of her sister's voice was both a balm to her anxiety and a catalyst for it. *Distraction, that's what I need.*

Winter showered and changed into the dress, drying her long hair and leaving it down. She applied a light touch of makeup and slid a long silver chain around her neck. Studying herself in the mirror critically, she saw none of the beauty in her face that people told her she had. To Winter, she just looked sad.

Stop. Stop wallowing in self-pity. She checked her watch then blew out her cheeks. It was time. She locked her houseboat and started down the jetty, surprised when she saw Raziel walking toward her. He grinned at her. "I thought it polite to escort you. I wasn't expecting you'd be on time."

"Personality flaw," she tried to make a joke to jolt herself out of her awkwardness. "Punctuality runs in the family."

Raz smiled down at her. "You'll have to tell me about your family over dinner."

Oh God. Winter made a noncommittal sound as Raziel offered her his arm as they walked back along the jetty and she took it hesitantly.

As they reached his yacht, with a slight nudge, Raz unexpectedly steered her towards a limousine, opening the door for her. "I thought I might take us somewhere a little... neutral."

Winter blinked then chuckled. "You keep surprising me."

"In a good way?"

She half-smiled. "That remains to be seen."

"You're a hard woman to please. I like that."

Winter didn't know how to respond to that, so she climbed into the backseat of the limo, shifting along the bench seat so he could join her. He was so tall, almost a foot taller than her five-five, that she felt dwarfed by him, and a little intimidated—not that she'd show it. Once again, he was impeccably dressed, the blue in his eyes brought out by the dark grey suit, his face clean-shaven. She had to admit, he was a good-looking man. Raz glanced at her, smiling at her scrutiny. "Did I pass the test?"

"I'm still considering."

She saw his eyes drop to her dress, and she tugged at it self-consciously. Sitting, the skirt hit her midthigh, and she wished she'd put on pantyhose or something.

"You look beautiful," Raziel said softly, and she flushed.

"I'm sure you're used to much more glamourous women."

"Glamorous, possibly. Beautiful? Not a chance."

Winter looked away from his intense gaze, embarrassed. He was a player alright, but there was something appealing about him nevertheless.

THE RESTAURANT TURNED out to be a surprisingly low-key affair in the center of the city. They were shown to a private booth which overlooked the Columbia river. The food was excellent and over the course of the meal, Winter found herself warming to the man opposite her.

Raziel was funny, erudite—cocky, for sure, and way too sure of himself—but he was respectful of her and seemed interested in her life. Winter gave him the basic details but didn't mention the shooting. She told him about Autumn—the news her sister was a celebrity chef was always a good way to distract someone from asking more difficult questions—and Raz was no different. "I have to say I'm not one to watch a lot of television, but I have heard of your sister. She's active in the New York social circle."

"She is." Winter sipped her wine and hoped he wouldn't question her on why she was so different from her outgoing sister.

"So," Raziel said casually, "would it be inappropriate for me to ask if there's someone special in your life?"

"You can ask," Winter shot back, "but I'm under no obligation to answer."

Raz threw his head back and laughed heartily. "God, woman, you are a ball breaker. I love it."

Winter grinned despite herself. "Not really, just very private. Let's make a deal. I'll tell you mine if you tell me yours."

Raz, still smiling, held out his hands. "I'm not going to pretend I'm a saint, Winter, but no, I'm not currently seeing anyone."

"Neither am I. But," she added, cautiously, "neither am I looking for a relationship."

Raz sat back and regarded her steadily. "Me neither. But I would like to fuck you, Winter Mai."

Winter choked on her mouthful of wine, and Raz grinned a little wolfishly. "Gotcha."

Winter wiped her mouth carefully, giving herself time to recover from the shock of his admission. Was he playing games with her? Did he mean it? What was worse? The fact he was so utterly sure of himself that he could say that or that her body had reacted in a way that shook her? Desire had flooded through her at his words, but Winter couldn't be sure if it was for this particular man, or that it had been so long since she let someone touch her, let alone make love to her?

She studied Raziel Ganz. Good-looking, sexy, and not looking for commitment. Was she the type of woman who would be some rich guy's fuck buddy?

Nope. "Mr. Ganz, I'm sure there are some women who would be impressed or even flattered by that kind of statement." Winter straightened her back. "I'm not one of them."

Raziel shrugged good-naturedly. "Fair enough. Winter, I'm not assuming anything. I spoke the truth, but just because I want you doesn't mean I get to have you. I know you can't be bought, and that's why I like you. Do me one favor?"

"What?"

"Keep the hamper. It would be such a waste."

Winter fiddled with her wine glass. "Fine. On one condition."

"Which is?"

She drew in a deep breath. "I don't mind the parties... just, please, no more fireworks."

"You don't like them?"

She shook her head, attempting a smile. "I don't. Loud, sudden noises... not a fan."

"Got it. Okay, deal... if we can do this again. Hang out, talk. I'm in Portland for a while... I'd like us to be friends."

Winter hesitated for a long moment before nodding. "Okay. You have a deal, Raziel Ganz."

AFTER RETURNING TO THE PIER, Raz walked her to her boat and kissed her hand. "Come and have drinks with me tomorrow night, if you would. Casual, I promise."

Winter nodded. "Okay. Goodnight, Raziel. Thank you for dinner."

"My pleasure, sweet one."

She watched him walk back to his yacht and wave back at her before disappearing into the vast boat. Winter went inside and locked the door after her, her emotions in turmoil. Did she really want another person in her life? Especially one like Raziel Ganz, who was obviously used to getting what he wanted, and he'd made it clear—he wanted *her*.

She had to admit that despite her misgivings, it was flattering, and jeez, it had been an age since she'd last been laid... almost three years now, before the shooting. Her college boyfriend, Kai, had been a sweet-hearted boy from Minnesota. After the shooting, he'd stayed around for her recovery, but she had been able to tell that he was freaked by the whole thing. Their relationship limped on for a few months with minimal contact before Winter had taken pity on him and set him free. She hadn't heard from him ever again, and she was strangely okay with that. He was from 'the before.'

She was still thinking about him and not concentrating when her phone buzzed, and distracted, she didn't check who it was calling.

"Winnie?"

Oh shit. "Auttie."

Her sister gave a relieved sigh. "Thank God. Thank you for picking up this time."

Winter didn't know what to say. Autumn had been calling and calling, not taking the hint—or rather, ignoring the fact she knew Winter wanted to be left alone. Typical Autumn. "How are you?"

"Really? That's all you have to say to me?" Autumn was quick to irritation. She liked to be in control, and that had always included her sisters. Summer had been the soft one, the peacemaker. "I haven't spoken to you in six months, Winter."

Winter sighed. "Fine. Look, there's no way I can make it home for Thanksgiving so..."

"Is it money? Because I can send you..."

"It's not the money." Winter tried not to snap at her sister, but she'd had this conversation over and over again. Autumn still thought most problems could be fixed by throwing money at them. She would get on well with Raziel, Winter thought to herself with a pang. Autumn outstripped on her younger sister on most things.

"Winnie... no one blames you for Summer. You have to stop thinking that we..." Autumn's voice broke off, and Winter heard her sister take a deep breath. "We love you; we miss you. It's like we lost both of you, Win."

Low blow. "I can't," Winter whispered. "I just can't." And she ended the call, switching off her phone.

All the buzz from her dinner with Raziel Ganz was gone now, and Winter sank to the floor of the boat, pulling her knees up tight to her chest. Pretending to be the companion of a rich guy so far out of her league? Yeah right. When she couldn't even face her own family, how was she supposed to pull that ruse off? She was a loner, and that was her life now. She would go and cancel tomorrow night and concentrate on getting through the week day by day.

Before she could change her mind, she scribbled a note to Raz and headed over along the jetty. His security guard, whose name she had learned was Davide, nodded at her. "Do you want to go up, Miss?"

Winter shook her head and gave him a hesitant smile. "No, thank you. Would you mind passing this note along to Mr. Ganz, please? I'd be very grateful."

Davide, a tall, broad man, nodded. "Of course, Miss... although I'm sure he'd like to see you."

"No. Thank you." She gave the man an awkward wave and walked back to her houseboat.

Inside, she stripped off her green dress, changed into her sweats, and fell into her bunk. Despite everything, Winter fell asleep, but the nightmares soon came and by the early hours she was shivering, caught somewhere between sleep and awakeness, whimpering, tears streaming down her face.

That's when she heard the girl scream.

CHAPTER SIX

Satchel opened the door to his apartment and grinned at his visitor. "Hey you. Thanks for coming."

Asha grinned at him. His ex-girlfriend, his love for so long, was now the one person he could say was his most trusted confident. Since their breakup, it seemed to Satch, they had become closer, seeming to realize they were always meant to be the best of friends instead of lovers.

Asha, a stunning Indian-American lawyer, hugged him, then patted his face. "Damn it, Satch, why do you get prettier as you get older? Jerk."

"Saddlebags."

Asha threw her head back and laughed. There was nothing saddlebaggish about Asha's incredible body and she knew it. She kissed his cheek. "Now that you're...ahem...sweet-talking me, I know you want something. Luckily, I brought wine—" she pulled two bottles of red wine from her bag "—and I took a cab here so we can get wasted."

Satchel laughed and went to fetch some glasses. "Well, you're right. I need a favor... I've been summoned to the big house for

Thanksgiving, and I wond—" He broke off as Asha made a face. "Uh-oh."

"Honey, you know normally I would, but... well, I've kind of been seeing someone."

Satchel raised his eyebrows. "Oh? How long has that been going on?"

Asha grinned. "You make it sound like high school, *Dad*. He's in shipping. Giovanni. You know how I like my Italians," she said winking at him, and he laughed.

A little pang of something still ached in his heart, but Satchel brushed it aside. He had no right to assume a gorgeous woman like Asha would stay single forever. She'd moved on, and in truth, in his heart, so had he, but he couldn't see a future where he would be with anyone again. "Well, I'm happy for you, Ash. I really am."

Asha beamed and uncorked the wine. "You would like him, Satch, I promise. So... why d'you need a wing man—wing *woman* —anyway?"

"Dad's on a tear. Worried that I haven't seen anyone since you and I split."

"Well, it is a little strange. Come on, Satch, you're gorgeous, rich, and a sweetheart. Those magazines that put you at the top of their most eligible bachelor polls have a point. Wait..." She dived into her tote bag again and pulled out a copy of Forbes, waving it triumphantly. "In this very issue." She flicked to a color spread and gave it to him.

Satchel saw his own image staring back at him and read through the puff piece quickly. "I sound like a douche bag."

Asha snorted. "You do not. Let's have a look at your competition."

For the next few minutes, Satchel chuckled as Asha bitched about the other men featured. Then a photograph caught his eye. "Hey, this guy." He tapped the photograph. "This dude, Ganz, has been calling the office. Wants a meeting with me."

"Really?" Asha made a face. "What does a shipping magnate want with an architect?"

Satchel grinned. "No idea. Seems pretty keen though. I have my suspicions that he's more interested in—"

"—getting close to your dad. Got it."

Satchel's father was a commissioner on the City of Portland Board. If Ganz wanted to bring his billion-dollar business to the city, he would need a good friend on the board to ease the passage of any permits he might need.

"Why go through me? Just call my dad." Satchel was a little irritated, then sighed. "Well, I guess it's too late now. I agreed to meet the dude."

Asha's eyes lit up. "You have a date? With a *billionaire*?" She giggled as he glared at her.

"Ha ha. I agreed to meet him; it doesn't mean I'm going to be doing him any favors. Anyway, my immediate problem is who I'm going to take to Thanksgiving, so Dad doesn't lose his mind over my bachelorhood."

"*Most eligible* bachelorhood." Asha amended. "Well, how would you feel about being set up with someone?"

Satchel grimaced. "God. Who?"

"There's a really sweet paralegal at my office. I say sweet, but I don't really know her; she seems nice. Single."

"How old?"

Asha grinned sheepishly. "About twenty."

"No. No. *No*. God, Ash..." Satchel grimaced. "I feel old."

"But you're a stud."

"No, Ash. *No* to the *only-just-out-of-her-teens* paralegal. I'm not *that* guy."

Asha looped her arm around his shoulders. "I know. It's just... I'm not sure I know who your type is. Do you?"

"Someone more my age, perhaps. But apart from that... no. I just can't see it."

"That's depressing."

"Tell me about it."

. . .

SATCHEL ENJOYED his evening with Asha and as she kissed his cheek and disappeared, he leaned against his door and blew out his cheeks. If Asha wasn't the one for him, who the hell would match up? He couldn't see how anyone could.

Face it, Satchel boy. It's TV dinners for one from now on.

He closed the door behind him and went to bed. The wine had gone to his head a little, and he lay in bed staring up at the ceiling. When he finally fell asleep, he dreamed of a woman smiling sweetly at him, holding out her hand to him, and the feeling made his subconscious react, pumping serotonin throughout his system.

It was only when he woke up that he recognized that his dream lover was Winter Mai.

The scream woke Winter from her troubled sleep, and she sat up in her bunk, her ears straining to hear any sound in the quiet night. All she could hear was the jingle of the rigging of the sailboats in the harbor. Had she imagined it?

Oh God. Hallucinations again? They had plagued her as she recovered from the shooting, hearing the screams as she and Summer had cowered behind the fountain in the shopping mall as the shooter continued his rampage.

Winter swung her legs over the side of her bunk and padded up onto deck. It was freezing now, early November, and she shivered as she listened. Nothing. Silence. Shit, she had imagined it. Winter rubbed her face and sat down on the small bench she kept on the deck, ignoring the cold. She'd stopped her counseling sessions soon after they started, finding it too painful to relive Summer's murder and her own terrifying experience, but maybe now it was time to try to effect a change in her life.

"I'm stuck," she thought, "and I'm the only one who can do something about it." She knew she wasn't ready to reunite with her family —not yet—but maybe she could start to put herself out there. She'd spend Thanksgiving with Joe and Cassie, maybe even retract her refusal of Raziel's invitation.

Maybe even...

The thought of being with somebody was strangely appealing,

especially if it was just sex and no commitment. Winter looked over to the boat and saw Davide pacing up and down on the jetty. Did the man ever sleep? Chewing her bottom lip, Winter suddenly hopped off her boat and ran along the jetty.

"Davide? Um... I don't suppose..."

Davide smiled at her—really, for a security guard he had the kindest face—and dug in his pocket and pulled her note out. "I wondered if you'd change your mind, Miss. Here you are."

Winter, flushing red hot, took her note back. "Thank you." She turned away and then turned back to him. "I'm not a golddigger, Davide."

"It's none of my business, Miss. None. Besides..." It was his turn to hesitate. "Mr. Ganz is an intelligent man. He has discerning taste." He smiled at her again. "He has good taste. Goodnight, Miss Mai."

She grinned gratefully at him. "Goodnight, Davide... and thanks."

"My pleasure."

Winter went home and sat on her bunk, the note in hand. So... tomorrow night she would join Raziel Ganz for private drinks on his yacht. That's all, drinks, she told herself fiercely, but shivered with anticipation at what else could happen when she was alone with him...

DAVIDE WATCHED the young woman go back to her houseboat and then made his way up to the darkened deck. Ganz sat in the darkness, smoking, watching the light in Winter's houseboat go out. Davide nodded at his boss. "Just like you said, boss. I gave her the note back."

Raziel smiled. "Good. Tell me, Davide, why is it these women think they can ever dictate the terms?"

"Don't ask me, boss."

Raz smiled coldly. "Doesn't matter. Winter Mai will soon learn she has no say in this thing. Listen, tell the cleaning staff to change the sheets in the master bedroom, would you, for tomorrow night? I have a feeling I won't be alone."

"Sure thing."

Davide started to walk away and then was called by back by Raz. "Davide... call the guy. Tell him we have another package for him; see if he can dispose of her body. And sack the guard who let her scream. They're supposed to be sedated... what the hell went wrong?"

"I've already fired him. The girl's body is already on its way to the bottom of the Pacific, boss, don't worry." Davide looked over at Winter's houseboat. "*She's* exquisite. Miss Mai. You'd get a good price for her."

Raz smiled triumphantly. "Oh, I have other plans for Miss Mai. There are some things that are priceless, Davide, and I have a feeling Winter Mai will prove to be one of them."

"And if she isn't?"

Raziel just smiled, but his eyes were cold and dead. "Let's hope, for her sake, she is."

CHAPTER SEVEN

S atchel had already agreed to attend the benefit in honor of his father, and so he was expecting the press outside the venue. It never got easier though as the paparazzi jostled for the best shot of the enigmatic billionaire, and Satchel wasn't in a mood to give them more than a couple of minutes. He'd pose for even less if it weren't for the fact this thing was for his dad, and he didn't want to seem surly or disrespectful tonight.

Inside the venue, he sought out his father and Janelle, who greeted him in a flurry of colored scarves and warm perfume. "Hello, Brat! Thank you for coming out tonight. Your dad's been bragging about you."

Patrick rolled his eyes. "As usual, she exaggerates. Now, son, I have someone I'd like you to meet."

Satchel groaned. "God, Dad, not another girl you want me to date..."

"No, don't worry." He looked around and nodded at a man Satchel's age. "Guy? Hey, Guy... Satchel, this is Guy Holbrook. He works out of New York.... Guy, this is my son, Satchel."

Satchel shook hands with the other man, studying him curiously. "Mr. Holbrook. What brings you to Portland?"

"A new business partnership, I'm hoping," Holbrook smiled. "I've been looking to invest in some land, and I know you are the guy to see in this town about designing state-of-the-art developments." He nodded at a beaming Patrick. "Your father has been telling me that every one of your buildings is an award winner. I'd be interested to see some of your work."

Satchel was surprised but nodded. "Of course. We'll arrange a meeting."

"Thank you."

THE REST of the party went off well, and Satchel was relieved that his father nailed his speech. Janelle and Satchel whooped as the rest of the gathering applauded his dad, and Satchel grinned as Patrick flushed bright red. Shyness was something the father and son shared.

Satchel had just said goodbye when he noticed a young woman approaching him. "Mr. Rose?"

She was tall and willowy with blonde hair and ice-blue eyes. Attractive, but there was something watchful about her, and when she introduced herself, Satchel realized why. "I'm Mallory Kline, Mr Rose."

Journalist. "Good to meet you, Ms. Kline, but I'm sorry, I'm not giving interviews at this time. Tonight is about my dad."

She smiled. "I know. I'm here off the record, off duty. I just thought I'd introduce myself." She looked around. "Are you going to offer me a drink?"

It took a moment for Satchel to realize she was hitting on him, and his heart sank. God, not this. Mallory Kline was beautiful, but he really wasn't in the mood. "Of course, I'm sorry." Satchel was unfailingly polite even if he wasn't interested. He beckoned the waiter over and grabbed a flute of champagne for the journalist.

Mallory thanked him with a smile. "You're not drinking?"

"I don't. Not for any moral reason; it's just that I'm driving."

Mallory smiled. "I heard that. I heard you always kept a clear head, so you could escape social situations quickly."

Satchel gave a half-shocked laugh. "And where did you hear that?"

"I have my sources. May I call you Satchel?"

"That's my name."

She nodded. "Thank you. Satchel, I'm not one for playing games, so I'm just going to come out with it. I'd like to do a profile. And by that, I don't mean the kind of puff piece like in Forbes. No putting you in the *Top Ten Most Fuckable Billionaires in America* lists. *You.* Hopes, dreams, passion, but also your nightmares; what haunts you. Why someone who looks like you is so reclusive. The whole shebang."

It was also an automatic response to say no to these types of things, but Mallory Kline's honesty stayed Satchel's tongue. "The ugly truth?"

"Yup. No matter how ugly." She studied him. "I'm guessing every instinct is telling you to throw me out right now, and that's exactly why I want to do this. You're a challenge, and men like you don't come along every day. Say yes, Satchel."

Satchel took a beat before he shook his head. "I don't think so, Miss Kline. But thank you for being so open."

Mallory shrugged and fished out a card from her purse and handed it to him. "Fair enough. But call me if you change your mind. Not wishing to blow smoke up my own ass, but I think I could help you."

"Help me help you?"

Mallory grinned. "*Quid pro quo*, Clarice." She got up and ever polite, Satchel stood and shook her hand. Mallory walked away and then turned back to him, smiling. "By the way... you'd be top of that list."

"What list?"

She laughed. "You're *definitely* the most fuckable billionaire I've ever met."

.   .   .

SATCHEL WAS FLATTERED, and that was a strange feeling for him these days. Maybe Asha and his dad were right; he should get back out there again.

Janelle came up behind him, slipping her arm through his. "Haven't we been the little social butterfly this evening? It's good to see, Brat. You're too much of a catch to waste away in your ivory tower, Satch. Your dad is right about that, at least."

Satchel grinned at his stepmother. "He was also damn right when he married you, Monster."

"Sweet boy. Pity you're a brat."

They both laughed as Patrick came to find them. Happy on booze and being feted, Satchel's dad hugged his wife and his son. "Love you guys. You're the best things that ever happened to me. Along with your mother," he said to Satchel hurriedly, and Satchel grinned.

"I know, Dad. It's okay. Listen, I'm going to take off."

He hugged his dad and stepmother goodbye and went out to find his car. Driving home to his empty, silent apartment, he put Mallory Kline's card on the breakfast counter and went to bed, wondering for the first time if he should call her. No to the interview, but maybe he should take her out.

For the first time in a long time, Satchel Rose went to bed and there was a glimmer of hope in his heart. The promise, the hope of something new...

THERE HAD BEEN a strange tension between Winter and Raziel since she'd arrived to spend the evening with him. It was as if they had both known what would happen that night and any conversation seemed to be laden with double meaning. They sat on the deck at a small table, candlelight flickering, and Winter felt as if her chest was constricted with the weight of sexual tension in the air.

Finally, Raz lifted her hand and kissed the back of her fingers. "Lovely one... we both know what's going to happen here tonight. Why do we need to put it off any longer?"

Winter was trembling with nerves, but she nodded, unable to

speak. Raz stood, gently pulling her to her feet and into his arms. He stroked her cheek then bent his head and kissed her.

His lips were gentle against hers at first, but as his hands slid into her long, dark hair, Winter felt his fingers tighten and grip her head. His kiss grew rough, his breathing ragged, his tongue insistent against hers. Raz gave a groan of desire as he released her, and they caught their breath. "Christ, you're exquisite..."

He swept her swiftly up into his arms and carried her beneath the deck to his state room. Winter didn't have the chance to study it before he laid her down on the bed and pushed her dress up over her hips. In one rapid move, Raz's fingers snagged the side of her panties and drew them down her legs.

"Wait... wait..." Winter's head was spinning, but then his mouth was on her sex, and she was gasping as his tongue lashed around her clit. It had all happened so quickly that she felt as if she weren't in control at all, but the electric sensations he was sending through her body made everything else fade away.

Before she could reach her peak, Raz left off and moved up her body, undoing the buttons of her dress and kissing every part of exposed skin. "I knew you'd be sensational," he murmured, kissing her throat and trailing his lips along her jaw. "Can you feel how much I want you, Winter Mai?"

Hesitantly, she slid her hand down to his groin, cupping his cock through his pants. Thick, heavy, and long against her palm, his cock stiffened as she touched him, and Raz gave a throaty laugh. "That's going to be inside you so soon, my beautiful little one."

She helped him undress, and then Winter stroked his cock against her belly, still nervous, but remembering what it was like to be held by a handsome man. Raz rolled a condom down over his straining cock and hitched her legs around his waist.

Winter gave a cry as he thrust hard into her, and for a delirious second, she wanted to scream at him to stop—that this was a mistake. Her emotions flooded her body with adrenaline and her eyes filled with tears.

Raziel noticed immediately. "Oh, my darling... did I hurt you?"

Winter shook her head, but she couldn't stop the tears from falling. "I'm sorry, I don't know what's wrong with me."

Raz withdrew and gathered her into his arms. He kissed her tenderly. "I was too rough."

"It's just been a while since I did this." Winter felt embarrassed, but Raz kissed her softly.

"It's okay, baby, we have all the time in the world." He ran his hand down over her body, pausing at each one of her scars. "What happened here?"

"An accident." It was her go-to-answer, one she'd used so often that it was automatic now. Winter really, really didn't want to have to explain anything to this man; she'd screwed—so to speak—the atmosphere, anyway. Goddamn it.

Raz stroked each scar and then her face. "Sweetheart... I know bullet wounds when I see them. Who in the hell would hurt you?"

She looked away from his gaze. "Like I said, it was an accident. I was lucky; other people died."

Raz nodded but didn't say anything else, and she was grateful for that. He kissed her again but the moment to make love had passed, and Winter felt like a failure. Christ, what was wrong with her? A handsome man was making love to her and she freaks out? *Jesus, you're one messed-up chick, Winter Mai.*

She felt like tears were imminent again, and she excused herself to go to the bathroom. Raz let her go to her relief, and she sat on the toilet, burying her head in one of the monogrammed hand towels and sobbing silently. *What a fucking mess...*

She calmed herself and splashed water on her face, not looking at her reflection in the mirror. Cautiously she went back into the bedroom. Raz had his pants on again, but he smiled at her, and wrapped her in a warm, plush robe. "Listen," he said gently, "I've ordered some food for us and taken the liberty of cueing up a movie for us to watch." He touched her cheek. "Movie night?"

It was such a sweet, such an unexpected gesture, that Winter wanted to cry again but instead she nodded. "I'd like that."

Still dazed by the sudden changes in atmosphere—all within an hour—Winter let herself be tucked into the crook of his arm as they sat on the bed. Food arrived soon, sea bass with asparagus, and they ate and talked about the movie, some old-time movie with Bette Davis. *Safe stuff,* Winter thought and was grateful to Raziel for the gesture of kindness and understanding. She had to admit—it showed his softer side, a side she wasn't sure he had.

She fell asleep at one point, and when she woke suddenly, blinking and disoriented, Raz was asleep, too, and she was cradled against his big chest. Winter gazed up at him; the hard lines of his gloriously handsome face were softened by sleep, and hesitantly, she traced the line of his lips with her finger.

Raz opened his eyes, and they were soft as he gazed back at her. Without speaking, Winter pressed her lips to his, felt him respond and tighten his arms around her. Raz rolled her onto her back and this time, they were a partnership, moving in complete synchronization as they began to make love.

This time she helped him roll the condom down over his cock, and he got her wet enough that when he finally entered her, there was no pain, no shock, and they moved together, kissing, caressing, even laughing with each other.

Raz was an expert lover, knowing how to bring her right to the point of orgasm, and then holding back to prolong the anticipation so that when she finally came, her back arched up, pressing her belly against his as she felt his cock pumping. Raz buried his face in her neck as he came, and she felt him bite down on her shoulder, felt the quick pain, but she didn't care.

They collapsed back on the bed, panting for air and laughing. "Now that's what I call movie night," Raz said, and she laughed.

"Yeah, that's the stuff." All of her earlier fears and doubts had disappeared. Raz kissed her, and she responded eagerly. Strange how quickly things could change.

It was late, and she glanced out of the window. "Maybe I should go home."

"Why? It's not like it's across the city; it's right there where you can see it." Raz propped himself up on his elbow and smiled down at her. "Stay. I'd like you to." He dipped his head and kissed her mouth. "I really would."

Winter hesitated, but it would seem strange to 'go home' when she was right next to it, anyway. "Okay... I would like that."

"I want to wake up with you," Raz said, his eyes serious, "You have enchanted me, Winter Mai."

She grinned at him. "Care to enchant me again?" She wiggled her eyebrows at him, and he laughed.

"You're Goddamn right I do..." He drew her to him, and they began to make love again, long into the night until finally they were exhausted.

RAZIEL OPENED his eyes and studied the woman so deeply asleep in his arms. Christ, she was beautiful, and a magnificent lay... *eventually*. He'd wondered why she had freaked out, but the scars on her body told him the story. Something happened to this little girl—the mall massacre—and obviously 'seriously injured' hadn't even covered it. From the looks of it, she'd been shot point blank, up close and very, *very* personal.

He could picture it, her lovely body jerking from the force of the bullets pumping into her. Jesus, how the hell had she survived? He touched each scar, the two on her chest: one below the collarbone, the other between her breasts. The four wounds on her belly, clustered around her navel. *Personal*, he thought again. She'd been lucky to survive. He splayed his hand over the scars on her belly and gazed down at her perfect face. "Don't ever make me hurt you like this," he whispered gently. "Don't make me hurt you, Winter."

He slipped from the bed and threw on his robe, glancing back at Winter's sleeping form before he left the bedroom and went to find Gareth.

As he expected, his night-owl assistant was still up, and he grinned at his boss. "How is the lovely Miss Mai?"

Raz smiled. "A *spectacular* fuck. Listen... I have a few things I want organized... quietly. Are you up for it?"

"Always." Gareth was always loyal, and he was well rewarded for it. "What's up?"

And grinning, Raz told him.

CHAPTER EIGHT

S atchel shook Guy Holbrook's hand. "Good to see you again. Look, I have a car outside. I thought, why waste time? You up for a little tour?"

Holbrook smiled and nodded. "Certainly."

Satchel drove to some of his favorite projects, and Holbrook asked all the right questions. Viewing the last project, one that was still in progress, a beachfront property with a private beach, Holbrook nodded approvingly at the half-built villa.

"This place got electric or Wi-Fi yet?"

"Not yet."

Holbrook smiled. "Good. Then there's no chance of anyone hearing what I'm about to say." He pulled something out of his pocket. "Mr. Rose... I haven't been honest with you. I'm not a property developer, I'm an agent with the F.B.I."

Satchel blinked. "What the hell?"

Holbrook showed Satchel his ID. "This is going to seem weird, and I apologize for the cloak and dagger, but I'm here to ask a favor from you from the agency."

"Am I in trouble?" Satchel was confused.

"Not at all, I assure you. I believe you've been contacted by a man called Raziel Ganz?"

Satchel frowned. "The shipping dude? Yes, he's been trying to set up a meeting with me. Just to grease the skids with my father, I think. What about him?"

Holbrook nodded. "We'd like you to keep that meeting. Get to know Ganz, work with him, whatever he wants."

"Because?"

"Because we believe Mr Ganz isn't who he says he is. Shipping is allegedly a cover for his actual line of business—and I use the word *allegedly* because we still haven't gathered enough proof to make a move on him. We believe he's at the top of a very long list of people who are trafficking young woman abroad to sell to the sex trade."

Satchel was shocked. "What the hell?"

Holbrook sighed. "As I say the investigation is at its earliest stages, but we need someone to be on Ganz's good side, and the fact he wants something from you means you're our guy. You can say no."

"And be responsible for more girls going missing? Jesus, man, this is a lot."

Holbrook looked sympathetic. "I know, and as I say, you are under no obligation. But so far, you are our only in. Satchel—I can call you Satchel?"

"Of course."

"Satchel, last night the body of a young woman was found on a beach just outside Portland. She had been stabbed to death. We identified her as a seventeen-year-old homeless woman who had been abducted from the streets three weeks ago. We think she was an illegal immigrant from the Far East. The injuries on her body... she died *hard*, Satchel, and her body, what was left of it, bore the marks of someone who had been starved and bound and tortured. We guess that she was abducted by people who were prepping her to sell on the internet. Guess when Ganz turned up in town?"

Satchel shook his head. "Surely someone that visible..."

"Oh, he doesn't do his own dirty work, of course, which is why we've had so much trouble getting any evidence on him. Satchel, it takes a lot for the Agency to ask a civilian to help us out. We wouldn't ask, but we're desperate to save any more girls from being taken. We need someone inside."

"So, what do you want me to do?"

"Keep the meeting with Ganz, offer to help. Befriend him. Get close."

Satchel's heart sank. "I don't know what you know about me, but I'm a pretty private guy. I don't make friends easily."

Holbrook nodded and seemed to hesitate. "I know what happened with Callan Flint. It wasn't your fault. The guy is crazy. There's a reason why he's in Western State Hospital. The judge would have sent him to prison for life instead of a high-security mental health facility if he wasn't."

Satchel sighed, wanting to change the subject desperately. "Look, even if I get close to Ganz, what is it you want me to do?"

"Stay close. Anything, anything that bothers you, you come to us. It might be the smallest thing, you never know, which could blow this case wide open. Sorry, I sound like a goddamned TV show." He grinned suddenly which made Satchel relax.

"Look, I'll meet with him, see what I think. Then I'll let you know whether I can help."

Holbrook nodded. "I appreciate it."

"I'm not saying yes yet."

"And you know..." Holbrook looked around the villa. "You are very talented. This will be spectacular when you've done."

Satchel relaxed a little. "Thanks. It's my pet project, my own place. Labor of love."

"Nice." Holbrook held his hand out, and Satchel shook it. "I really do appreciate you taking the time, Satchel. This is an important case. *My* labor of love, you could say. Too many young women have had their lives snatched away by these people. I want to take them—and Ganz—down."

It was a couple of days before Satchel asked Molly to set up his meeting with Raziel Ganz. In the meantime, he'd been thinking about Callan, what he could have done to stop his friend from losing it and killing all those people. Maybe he could ease some of his own guilt if he helped the F.B.I.

He'd researched Ganz—the man was a few years Satchel's senior —and on the surface a respectable, self-made billionaire. In shipping terms, he was right at the top of the tree, his business based out of New York. So, what did he want in Portland? And why did he want to meet with Satchel if it wasn't to get to Patrick?

Molly came back to him and said Ganz had invited him to a cocktail party on his yacht that Friday. Satchel sighed. More socializing, but he nodded and told Molly to confirm. He called Holbrook on the burner phone Holbrook had sent him and told him about the party.

"It's probably a good idea," Holbrook told him. "It'll give you the chance to observe him, see who he's hanging out with. Satchel, I'm grateful for your help. I've been trying to take Ganz down for years. This may finally be the time."

So NOW AS he drove towards the harbor, Satchel concentrated on what Holbrook had told him. Watch, observe, judge. He parked his car and walked down the jetty, past the moored sailboats and the few houseboats on this side of the harbor. Ganz's yacht stood out, huge, white, and lit up for the party. Satchel grimaced. Why people thought parties were *fun* was beyond him, but he'd made his bed and now he had to lie in it. He was greeted by a burly bodyguard who apologized as he patted him down. "Just a formality, sir."

"Of course, no problem."

The bodyguard stood aside, and Satchel walked up the gangway. As he moved onto the deck, he headed straight for the drinks table and helped himself to a flute of champagne to steady his nerves. He scanned the gathering for his host—clearly the guy wanted to make an entrance.

Twenty minutes later, Satchel was proved correct as Raziel Ganz arrived on deck, dressed in a designer suit, his arm around the waist of one of the most exquisitely beautiful women Satchel had ever seen.

His heart began to thump wildly as he recognized her, and he felt the blood drain from his face. No, it couldn't be... what the hell was she doing here, and what the hell was she doing with Ganz?

Satchel stared at her as Winter Mai smiled shyly up at Raziel Ganz, and he kissed her directly on the mouth.

CHAPTER NINE

Winter still felt whiplashed by the speed that her relationship with Raziel Ganz had heated up. They spent every night together; Winter hadn't slept in her own bed for a week now, and she had to admit, the sex was addictive.

Raziel was a skilled lover, and the obvious admiration of her body that he displayed was flattering. He did not share a lot of who he really was, but for Winter, that was just fine at the moment. She liked him, but in her heart, she knew she could never fall for him. He was a million miles from what she wanted, but for right now, he was just what she needed.

And she felt herself becoming more open to the world, even in such a short time. She still got nervous when she went out into the world, but even Joe had commented this week on her lifting of spirits. "It's good to see, Win. You're too special to hide yourself away."

Raziel would work during the day, and to his credit, he wasn't one of those men who expected her to be at his beck and call. He would call around supper time and invite her to eat with him, and sometimes Winter would invite him to her houseboat. He would come, bearing some sort of gift—food, wine, or flowers usually—dressed casually, and he would think nothing of sharing a plain bowl of pasta and tomato sauce with her. There was only something slightly incongruous about this billionaire slumming it with her.

And now, as she stood with him greeting his party guests, Winter knew he had come into her life for a reason, to set her free again. She was still shy and was aware of his friends' curious looks at her, wondering who she was.

AN HOUR INTO THE PARTY, and as she saw Raz deep in conversation with a glamourous-looking couple, she took the opportunity to excuse herself and find a quiet corner to breathe and regroup. The far end of the deck was in darkness and she sank down thankfully, perching on top of a small bench. She blew out her cheeks and then started as she heard a quiet voice.

"Hiding out? Me, too."

She peered into the dark and saw a man leaning over the side of the ship. He stood up and stepped into the light, and Winter's stomach gave a flip. He was, without doubt, the most beautiful man she had ever seen. Dark, almost black hair, in a shock of curls around his head, and dark, thick eyelashes rimmed the most remarkable green eyes she had ever seen. He smiled, crooked, sweet, his eyes soft, and Winter felt her entire body react. In that moment, she knew her feelings—whatever they were—for Raziel could never be more than casual.

The man held out his hand. "Hello."

"Hi." She shook it, feeling the warm, dry skin on hers. *Pull me into your arms, kiss me...*

The man nodded towards the party. "I'm not much for these things. I'm a geek, unfortunately, more at home with a book."

"Nothing wrong with that." Her heart was thumping so hard she was sure he could hear it. "I'm the same. My idea of heaven would be a good book, a quiet place..."

"... with a dog curled at your feet."

Winter nodded. "Perfect."

They smiled at each other, and Winter felt the connection building. She opened her mouth to ask him his name, but then she heard Raziel calling her. She stood as Raz came around the corner, carrying two flutes of champagne. He smiled and kissed her cheek. "Darling, I wondered where you were." He handed her a glass and then smiled at the stranger. "Mr. Rose, I see you've met my partner, Winter Mai. Winter, this is Satchel Rose. I very much hope to be working with him whilst I'm in Portland."

Winter felt the shock hit her with the force of a thousand bricks. *This* was Satchel Rose? The best friend of the man who murdered her sister, who had shot her in cold blood?

Satchel Rose was looking at her with those beautiful green eyes, but all she could think of was her sister, her blood gushing from the bullet wound on her throat, and Winter felt the rage, the pain build up, and she did the only thing she could think to do in that moment.

She threw her drink in Satchel Rose's face.

CHAPTER TEN

"What the *fuck* was that?" Raziel was incensed. Later, in his bedroom, he ranted while an unrepentant Winter sat and listened. After the emotion of earlier, she felt nothing except empty.

"Do you even know who that man could be to me? To my business? Jesus, Winter..." He was angrier than she had ever seen him. His eyes were hard as he looked at her. "Are you even sorry?"

"No."

Raz grabbed her wrists and pulled her to her feet. A note of fear crept into her then. "Raz, you're hurting me."

"I don't give a fuck. You could have ruined everything, *everything*, Winter." He released her wrists then, seemingly to understand he was going too far. He ran a hand through his short hair, his mouth a thin line of anger. "Why? Why did you do it?"

Winter drew in a deep breath and unbuttoned her dress. Raz held out his hands. "As gorgeous as you are, you can't distract me with sex this time."

This time? "I hadn't realized I *distracted* you with sex before. I'm trying to answer your question." Her voice was icy. She pulled open her dress. "You asked me what these were. Three years ago, I was shot six times by a man named Callan Flint in the St Anne's Mall Massacre. I'm sure you've heard of it; it was national news.

Callan Flint is or was Satchel Rose's best friend. He testified for him in the court case. Callan Flint murdered my sister Summer right in front of me. He shot her in the throat, and she bled out in front of me, in agony, in terror. Then he stood over me and shot me at point blank range. That's why I threw my drink in Rose's face."

She pulled her dress shut. "I'm sorry if my sister's murder is *inconvenient* to your business aspirations, Raziel, but no, I don't regret what I did in the least. That bastard—" She broke off. Why did calling Satchel Rose a bastard make her feel so bad? It was in direct opposition to how she had acted, to what she was saying now. *It isn't just because of his soft green eyes, is it?* She took a deep breath. "Maybe this is a bad idea. Maybe we want different things, Raz." She buttoned up her dress. "I should go."

She walked to the door but Raz put an arm firmly across it. She looked up at him, alarmed, but his eyes were soft. "I'm sorry, baby. Please don't go. I'm sorry I was mad; I didn't know."

Raz slid his arms around her waist and bent his head to kiss her tenderly. "Please don't go, Winter, my darling. I hate the thought of you being hurt, and I'm sorry, so sorry about your sister." He nuzzled her nose with his own before kissing her again.

It took a few moments for Winter to unfreeze, but she leaned into his big body. "I'm sorry, too. I had no idea I would react like that."

Raz closed the bedroom door and picked her up in his arms, laying her down on his bed. "It's okay, I understand now." He unbuttoned her dress and kissed each one of her scars. "You're a survivor, Winter. I love that about you."

He hooked his fingers in her panties and drew them down her legs. "I'm a lucky man."

He covered her body with his, kicking off his shoes and getting rid of his shirt. Winter ran her hands over his hard chest as he kissed her, and soon he was inside her and they were making love.

Winter closed her eyes as he sucked on her nipples and an image of Satchel Rose flew into her mind. *No. Stop thinking about him. He is the enemy...*

But she still couldn't stop the fantasy that it was the gorgeous, shy Rose who was making love to her, and when she came, she came harder than she ever had.

Raziel seemed triumphant as he too reached his peak, and Winter felt a horrible guilt in her chest. What the hell was she doing? This handsome man was making love to her, and she was thinking about one of the two men in the world that she hated the most?

Those green eyes, those dark thick long lashes...

Stop.

Raz groaned as he came, and it was only then that she realized that, for the first time, they hadn't used a condom.

Oh God, no...

Only after Raziel had finally fallen asleep, his big, heavily muscled arms caged around her, did Winter finally give into her emotions and cry herself to sleep.

SATCHEL DROVE HOME, his suit still wet from the champagne Winter Mai had thrown on him, and he felt, not anger, but a strange kind of relief. She had every right to do that to him, but there was also the feeling that, despite her anger, something had happened between the two of them in the moments before Raziel Ganz had interrupted them.

It had taken all of his self control not to kiss her; all the emotions from his hospital vigil with her as she lay in a coma after the shooting returning to him: holding her tiny hand, watching her breathing with the help of the machines. Seeing her now, so alive, so vital, so achingly beautiful... God, it made his heart soar.

But... she was with Raziel Ganz, and that terrified Satchel. What the hell was she doing with that man? If Agent Holbrook was right, Ganz was a dangerous guy. Was Winter in danger of being sold into sex slavery? The fact Ganz was willing to be seen in public with her was a good thing; it would be harder to explain away if Winter went missing.

Unless of course, the rest of his party 'guests' had been in his employ—Satchel hadn't recognized any of them from Portland social circles. *Damn it...*

What was Winter doing in Portland? Satchel knew her family to be in New York: her surviving sister and her aunt, the woman who had brought the three Mai sisters up after their parents had been killed in a car wreck. The shooting had been in Seattle; Callan chose his killing ground at random.

Callan. His friend was rotting away in a mental health facility, and one of his victims was in the hands of an alleged human trafficker. What a fucking mess.

What the hell are you going to do about it, Rose? He shook his head. He knew he shouldn't interfere, but he owed it to Winter Mai to make sure she was safe. The more people who knew she was in Portland the better, but what could he do?

Back home, he stripped and showered, trying not to think about her sweet face and those lips he so wanted to kiss. The hard thing was he imagined the life they could have together, and that was ridiculous. She *hated* him. There wasn't any chance they would ever have the kind of future he was dreaming of: love, fun, laughter, two point five children, a pack of dogs, a house he built just for her.

That was a fantasy—a mad, ridiculous fantasy. He didn't know her—not really—and anyway, to her, he was the enemy, the friend of her attacker, of her sister's killer.

Oh goddamn it. Satchel tried to go to sleep but instead lay staring up at the ceiling. If he, Satchel, had never come to terms with what happened, how could he expect Callan's victims to?

He turned onto his side, unable to stop thinking about her dark eyes and soft skin. *Winter...* Maybe there was a way he could help her, make amends. He would never accept that he wasn't partially to blame for Callan's actions; how could he, the person closest to his friend, not have noticed the madness within?

And Winter in a relationship with Raziel Ganz... suddenly he had a brainwave. The more people who knew about Winter, knew her story, knew she was with Ganz, the more likely Ganz would not risk harming her or trying to sell her into sex slavery. Winter clearly didn't know who she was dealing with. She was so tiny, such a petite woman, that she looked utterly defenseless against Ganz's powerful presence. The thought that she was sleeping with him...

Ugh. She's not your property just because you held her hand once, douche bag. "I know, I know," Satchel murmured back at himself. But he hadn't been wrong about that instant attraction between them.

Satchel groaned and shoved the pillow over his head. *Stop thinking about her.*

But he knew then that he never would.

CHAPTER ELEVEN

"Well this is an unexpected surprise. I thought you would never call me." Mallory Kline's eyes crinkled as she grinned at him over her cup of coffee.

Satchel felt only a twinge of guilt as he smiled back. Clearly, Mallory Kline was gorgeous and hot for him, but it was her journalistic talents he needed now. The idea had come to him when he woke up that morning, and he'd spent the entire day arguing with himself. Was invading Winter's privacy a necessary price to pay for protecting her? Fuck it. He didn't care. Nothing was going to happen to that sweet girl while he could do something about it.

Even if he had to give up his own privacy. He had called Mallory, asked her to meet him for a late coffee. "I think I can give you the story you want."

Now, Mallory prompted him. "So, was that a ruse to see me, or do you actually have a story to tell?"

Satchel drew in a deep breath. "A story. *The* story. Callan, me, and what happened at the St. Anne's Mall. The victims... one in particular."

He saw a faint flicker of disappointment in her eyes—she obviously wanted to fuck him—but then her instincts kicked in. "You're really willing to talk about that? Now?"

He nodded. "For her. For the victim I was talking about. She's in trouble and..."

"Oh wow. You're in love with her." Mallory's eyes widened, but Satchel shook his head.

"No, I'm not." *Liar.* He swallowed, pushing the thought away. "I don't even really know her, but I do know she's in terrible danger, and she doesn't realize it."

"Then why not just tell her?"

Satchel smiled sadly. "Because she hates me. She wouldn't believe me if I told her."

"Told her what?"

"*That,*" he said, firmly, "I can't tell you. Or anyone. That's a deal breaker. I'll tell you my story and some of hers, enough to pique your interest and make you want to find out more about her."

Mallory shrugged. "The victims' stories have been told again and again. Why would this girl's be any different?"

"Because I can't find any trace that her story was told, and there's a reason why."

"There is?"

Satchel smiled. "She's Autumn Mai's sister."

That got Mallory's attention. "You must be crazy. Autumn lost her other sister in that massacre. She's made it absolutely clear that no one is to go near her remaining sister, or she'll throw their publication out of anything she has going on in New York."

"But your paper isn't in New York," Satchel said with a smile.

"True." Mallory considered. "Okay, but I want full access to you. Not just about Callan Flint, although anything you can give me there will help."

"Fine." Satchel swallowed the faint nausea he felt at using his old friend like this. "But I want Winter's name in the press, what she's doing, where she is." He sipped his coffee. "Who she's seeing."

Mallory studied him. "You *do* like her, but I have a feeling she won't love you for exposing her. There's a reason she went to ground. She'll be angry at you."

"I can cope with that." *If it keeps her safe...*

Mallory shook her head. "What is this, Satchel? I don't get why you think you owe this girl anything."

Satchel felt hollow as he met the journalist's gaze. "Because I owe her *everything*."

WINTER WOKE up before Raz the morning after the disastrous party and quietly dressed before leaving the yacht and going back to her houseboat. She let herself in with a sigh of relief, glad of the solitude. After making love with Raz last night—no, it wasn't making love, she thought now. That would involve having feelings, and she knew now that she could never feel anything but friendship, if that, for Raziel Ganz. The effect on her body of just being *near* Satchel Rose... even as much as she hated him, she couldn't deny it.

Winter sat down hard on the sofa and put her head in her hands. What a fucking mess. She'd screwed up her perfect quiet little life royally and for what? Sex. Great sex, yes, but with a man she knew she could never love.

What the hell is wrong with you?

Winter went to the bathroom, stripped down and stepped into the shower. She had a student at eleven a.m., and afterward, she intended to walk into the city, find a bookshop, and hunker down for an hour or so—get away from the area. Somehow, she didn't want to be around Raz today and the imposing presence of his luxurious yacht. She didn't belong there.

She let the water flow down her limbs, and when she was drying herself, her eye was caught by a small pill bottle. Antidepressants. She hadn't taken them for months now; they made her foggy even if her mood was lifted, but right now she could do with a Band-Aid, a walking stick, a crutch.

She picked the bottle up, considering, idly running her eyes over the instructions. *Consult your doctor if you think you are or might be pregnant...*

Shit. She remembered about the forgotten condom and cursed slightly. The chances were slim, yes, that she'd conceived from just that one time but not impossible. How long did it take for a pregnancy to show on a test?

She went into her bedroom and grabbed her laptop, opening the search engine. She sighed when she saw the answer to her question: six to eight days for a urine test. There was no way she could afford to go to a doctor. She wondered how much emergency contraception would cost her? Up to sixty dollars, the internet told her. *Goddamn it.* She grabbed her purse and checked her wallet. Sixteen dollars and thirty-three cents. After her student, she would have another hundred dollars, but then she had to make that last for food and bills for God knows how long.

Fuck. The vague idea of calling Autumn and asking her for a loan passed through her mind, but she dismissed it. Winter got up and dressed and went into her living room.

She gave a yelp of alarm when she saw a figure sitting on her couch. "Hello," Raz said pleasantly, but there was no warmth in his eyes. "I missed you this morning."

Winter took a deep breath, calming herself. She was absolutely sure she had locked the door behind herself. "I didn't want to wake you. I have a student in twenty minutes."

She looked away from his intense gaze, and he stood and drew her into his arms. "I hope you're not still mad about last night, darling. It was just... I need Rose on my side and I lost my temper. I'm sorry."

"You don't have to apologize, I was the one who lost her temper."

"With justification."

Winter sighed. "I thought so at the time. Now... it's not as if he was the one with the gun, Raz." She looked up at him. "Listen, I've been thinking we should... maybe just cool off for a time. I need to look for more clients and more work, and I'm sure you have—"

"I'm not letting you go, Winter."

His words, however lightly said, made a shiver pass up her spine. "Excuse me?"

Raziel smiled. "Sorry, that came out wrong. I mean... when we started this, neither of us wanted a relationship. But I'm not a stupid man. I know when I have the right woman in my arms. I'll fight for you, Winter. I mean it." He bent his head and kissed her, but she turned her head at the last moment and his lips pressed against her cheek.

Winter gave him a half-smile to soften the slight. "Let's talk later, can we? My student will be here any moment and I have to set up."

"Of course." He kissed her again, this time aiming for her cheek, and walked to the door. "By the way, this door is tricky. I can have one of my men take care of it if you like?"

She sighed inwardly but nodded. "Thank you." It wasn't like she could afford to have it fixed herself. Raz smiled at her and was gone. She closed the door behind him, running her fingers down the edge. It was rough, almost as if someone had forced the door open. She shivered. *Don't get paranoid.*

Luckily her student, a young teen named Phoebe, turned up, and Winter was distracted; thankfully, her spirits were lifted by the lesson. After Phoebe had left, Winter sat down at the piano herself and lost herself in playing for a few hours.

When she had been at college, she had studied to become a concert pianist, and then after graduation, she and Kai had moved to New York to be near her family as they sought positions in orchestral companies. They had both found work: Winter in a small company, Kai as a deputy music director for the New York State Ballet Company. They had been happy; she had been happy—as happy as she had ever been. Then came the day when her sister, her beloved Summer, had invited her to come with her to Seattle for a week.

Winter closed the piano lid and squeezed her eyes shut. Just one decision. To go shopping in the mall or to go see a movie. She couldn't even remember which movie. Shopping had won, even though Summer herself had her own retro clothing store. Summer— God, she had been so aptly named by their hippie parents—had linked arms with her younger sister, and they wandered around, mostly window shopping, laughing and talking.

And in a blink, it was over.

Winter pushed away from the piano and grabbed her purse. *Stop damn wallowing in the past, Mai.* She locked the door and glanced over at the Ganz yacht. Why did she feel uneasy about it now? It was just a damn argument. Maybe it had been the way Raz had reacted, grabbing her wrists. They were still sore.

She shook her head and set off for her favorite bookstore. The barista of the coffee bar at the back of the store greeted her, offered up her usual Earl Grey tea, and Winter smiled at him gratefully.

"Here you go, Win. Oh, hey man." The barista, Rich, smiled at someone behind Winter.

"Hey, Rich."

Winter froze. No way. It couldn't be; it was too much of a coincidence. Deliberately she picked up her mug, leaving the money for it on the counter and turned in the opposite direction. She fled for her usual seat, a small snug corner tucked away from the sight of the rest of the store and hid. Only then did she peek around the corner to see if Satchel Rose had noticed her.

There was no reason why he should have; with her back turned, she looked like any other girl with long dark hair. She saw him chatting with Rich and to her relief, he took his coffee and disappeared from view.

Winter took out her book but found it difficult to concentrate when any moment, she expected Satchel Rose to poke his head around the corner and confront her. She finished her tea, and after an hour gave up, thinking that the coast must be clear by now.

She wandered over to check out the shelf of new releases and soon lost herself in reading the blurbs on the back of them. There were a few customers in the shop at midafternoon, but Winter enjoyed these times most, when most people were at work, and she could think and breathe without too many people around.

"I thought it best to stay away from you whilst you had liquids to hand. Especially *hot* liquids."

Winter slowly turned, her face burning. Satchel Rose was smiling —a nervous smile to be sure—but still sweet enough to make her stomach flutter. Winter braced herself. "Mr. Rose."

"It's good to see you."

She raised her eyebrows in surprise—then, to her own shock— she burst out laughing. Satchel chuckled softly. "That," Winter managed to get out, "I *wasn't* expecting." She studied him. "Look, I'm sorry that I threw the drink on you last night. It was..."

"You don't have to apologize for anything, Miss Mai. Anything. I should have told you who I was right from the start."

Winter nodded. "Winter. My name is Winter."

"I know. Satchel. Satch." He held out his hand, and she took it, once again feeling how small her hand felt in his—his warm, dry skin, and that jolt of something undefinable that passed between them... *again.*

"Can I buy you another drink? I won't be offended if you say no under the circumstances."

Winter hesitated, staring at him. God, he was so beautiful with those green eyes, that dark hair. "Okay." She found herself saying it automatically. What harm could it do?

All of her anger and shock at finally meeting him seemed to dissipate as they walked back to the coffee bar. Rich grinned when he saw them together, but when Winter shot him a glare, he smoothed out his features and took their order.

They sat down at a different table from her snug, for which Winter was grateful. The snug was tiny, and she would have been squashed up against him.

Satchel Rose was tall, even taller than Raziel, and broad in the shoulder, and God, did he make a navy blue sweater work for him. His dark hair was messy, his dark brows heavy, and his eyes... God, those eyes.

Winter was aware she was staring and looked down at her drink, suddenly tongue-tied. She wanted to be so mad at this man... but he was nothing like the person she had built up in her head.

"Listen," he started now, "let's get the hard stuff out of the way. I'm so sorry. God, I'm so sorry about what happened to you, your sister, all those people. I still have a hard time believing it."

Winter swallowed the lump in her throat. "He was your friend."

"Yes." His beautiful eyes were troubled. "He was, and I wish, I wish I could tell you that there was some sign of what he would do. But there was nothing. I know you must hate me for testifying on his behalf, but I simply told the truth. There was nothing to suggest he would do... what he did."

Winter looked away from his steady gaze. After a beat, she shook her head. "I don't hate you. I don't know what I feel except... empty. Summer died in my arms. My sister. She was the good one, you know—the sunshine. It should have been me."

"No, don't say that." Satchel reached out and covered her hand with his. "It shouldn't have been either of you. Or any one of those victims. I keep going over and over it in my head. He didn't drink; he didn't do drugs; he showed no sign of mental illness. I knew him since we were kids, Winter."

Winter heard the heartbreak in Satchel's voice, and her heart ached for him. He had lost someone he loved, too, and she had never even considered that. Without thinking, she turned her hand over and linked her fingers with his. It seemed the most natural thing to do.

They sat in silence for a while, just holding hands. Winter smiled suddenly. "This is so weird."

Satchel chuckled. "Right? Still... I'd like us to be friends."

Winter nodded slowly. "It might take some time for that... not that I blame you, but for the last three years, I've been raging, hating, so fucking—excuse my potty mouth—but so fucking *angry* all the time. When I met you yesterday, before I knew who you were... there was a moment when I felt... happiness. And that's such a strange sensation for me now. And it was so silly, just you talking about reading, escaping, and then you mentioned the little dog, and in that second, you painted a picture of the life I want."

She felt her eyes filling with tears. "And I felt it. You *got* me."

Satchel's fingers squeezed hers. "I felt it, too."

Winter let out a shaky breath. "And then it all came crashing down on me, and I did what I did." She frowned at him. "In my head, I can't reconcile *you*—" she gestured to him, her expression confused, "with the Satchel Rose whose name I saw on court documents and in the papers and..." She stopped, wiped a tear from her face, and gave a strangled half-laugh. "It's... unfair. I know that sounds crazy."

"No, I get it. It *is* unfair." Satchel looked away from her for a moment. "And you're with Raziel Ganz."

Winter shook her head, and gently withdrew her hand from him, feeling immediately bereft. "No. We're just friends..." God, that was a lie, wasn't it? And somehow, she didn't want to lie to this man. "It's complicated."

"I see."

"He was pissed I threw that drink on you. He thinks I ruined his chances of doing business with you." She gave him a crooked smile, but Satchel frowned.

"He got angry with you?"

"Briefly. It was nothing, but you'd be doing me a huge solid if you still met with him."

Satchel nodded. "Consider it done." He paused. "You know much about his business?"

"Shipping? Not a thing. I'm a pianist and I live on a houseboat. Raz lives in an entirely different world." As she said it, the truth of what she was saying hit her hard. What was she doing with Raziel Ganz? Jesus, she was playing in a world that she had no right to be in.

And Satchel was in that world, too. Both men were way, way out of her league. She gave him a weak smile, trying not gaze at the way his thick eyelashes swept down to his cheek when he blinked, or the way his eyes softened when he gave her that sweet, crooked smile.

"I have to go," she said softly, and he nodded. He stood and kissed her cheek—even the feel of his lips against her skin made her close her eyes, and her heart ached for what could have been.

"Winter, I'll meet with Raz and smooth the waters, don't worry about that. But, can I ask a favor in return? Let's do this again. Coffee. Next week?"

Winter smiled. "Same time, same place?"

"I look forward to it."

She felt him watching her as she walked away, and at the door to the bookstore, she turned and smiled at him. He raised his hand and gave that smile that made her stomach twist with desire. She waved and fled, away from this man, this sweet man who for so long had been the focus of her hate, and she knew her life had changed immeasurably in the space of a few hours.

She didn't even realize she was crying until an elderly woman she was passing asked her if she was okay.

CHAPTER TWELVE

Two days later, it was Thanksgiving Day, and although Winter had cried off spending the last two nights with Raziel, he asked her to have drinks with him before she left for Joe and Cassie's house. Winter had come home the previous day to find her door fixed and a set of spare keys left for her.

"I hope that was okay," Raziel told her when she went to thank him the next morning. "I felt bad for breaking in on you."

"It's okay," she said carefully.

"Oh, and I hear I have you to thank? Satchel Rose called me, told me you'd run into each other at a bookstore in the city. Told me you asked him to honor his meeting with me." He raised his coffee cup to her. "Thank you, darling. I appreciate it."

"Well, it was my fault for almost blowing your meeting, so I'm glad I had the chance to put things right."

"I'm surprised. You have a pretty good reason not to speak to the man."

Winter sucked in a breath. "Well, maybe... just maybe I was taking it out on the wrong person."

Raziel studied her. "You know, if you want... I could make enquiries."

"What do you mean?"

"About Flint. There are ways he could be made to—"

"Don't even finish that sentence." Winter was shocked. Really, this is what having wealth and power was? He was actually offering to have Callan Flint killed?

Raz chuckled. "I was going to say he could be made to serve a more severe sentence. Really, Winter, what do you think I am?"

She blew out her cheeks. "Sorry. Drama queen tendencies." She joked to relieve the tension but still she couldn't shake the feeling that Raz meant exactly what she thought he had.

Raziel reached out and cupped her cheek but withdrew his hand when she gave an involuntary flinch. His eyes turned a dark grey. "What is it, darling?"

"I'm sorry, I'm out of sorts."

"I can take the day off, and we can spend time together if you want?"

"No, don't do that. I have two students today, and I need to get some sleep tonight. I'm having trouble." She looked down at her hands. "Raz, I have a great time with you, don't get me wrong, but I meant what I said at the start. I'm not looking for a relationship."

Raziel smiled. "We'll see."

His response annoyed her, but she held her tongue. She stayed to have breakfast with him but then made her excuses and left. She felt him watching her as she walked back down to the jetty to her home and wondered, for the first time, whether she should move her boat away from her mooring point. There were vacant spots, but it cost money to move.

Here, though, she felt exposed and observed. *That damn paranoia again.* She went back home and locked herself in, deciding to spend the morning spring cleaning until her students arrived.

The next day, Joe called to confirm she was still joining them. "Look, I have to bring something... maybe I could make a dessert? I make a mean peach cobbler."

Joe chuckled. "Cassie will love you for that. It's her favorite, but it's never the same when you make it yourself. Yeah, sure, that'll be good."

As she walked to the farmer's market, Winter thought about her coffee date with Satchel Rose. She had to admit, she could hardly wait to see him again, and yet something inside of her rebelled against the idea. She cursed herself a little for changing her opinion of him so quickly, so completely, just because he smiled that smile at her—just because his eyes made her weak, his presence, even his clean scent, made her head spin with desire.

She felt disloyal to Summer even considering being Satchel's friend. Thinking of Summer made her wonder if she should call Autumn and her aunt to wish them a happy Thanksgiving even if she couldn't bring herself to go see them. Not that she could afford the travel money.

Winter sighed and distracted herself by picking the fruit for the dessert. At the register, a headline in the paper caught her eye.

Third Homeless Illegal Immigrant Murdered.

The photograph showed a young woman, not older than twenty, Winter guessed. The girl was Asian, pale and beautiful, and Winter picked up the paper and read through the story quickly.

A third young Asian immigrant woman was found stabbed to death and dumped into the Columbia River. The unnamed victim was reported living on the streets of Portland after entering the United States illegally. The murder comes only a few days after the murders of two other young homeless women. Although there are no witnesses to the murder, residents of the harbor reported a woman's scream on the night she disappeared.

Winter blinked in shock. The date was the same evening she had heard the scream in the dead of night. She hadn't imagined it. "Fuck," she breathed, wondering if she should go to the police and tell them she, too, had heard it. But what else could she add? Nothing.

"Hey, you want that newspaper?"

Winter looked up to see the cashier waiting for her. She nodded, distracted, and paid for her stuff, thanking the cashier as he packed her bag for her.

"No problem." His smile was as insincere as his words, and as

Winter turned away, he muttered something under his breath that made her freeze.

"What did you say?" She was incredulous. The cashier smiled back at her.

"Nothing. Have a good day."

Winter glared at him and strode out of the store. She'd heard exactly what racial slur he'd called her, and it made her blood boil. Not that she wasn't used to it, but to be so flagrant about it...

She was still steaming when she got home, and the fact Raziel was sitting on her deck, smoking a cigar didn't improve her mood. Did he think he could just invite himself over when he wanted?

"I was hoping I could spend at least some of Thanksgiving with you," he said amiably as he followed her into the house. Winter dumped her shopping on the counter, not looking at him.

"I told you, I'm with Joe and Cassie for most of the day."

"But you won't be staying the night there, will you?"

Winter sighed. "No. But, Raz, I meant it when I said this isn't a relationship. We have fun, yes, and I enjoy your company very much, but..."

In a flash, he had her pressed up hard against the breakfast counter, his mouth seeking hers. Winter didn't have time to prepare herself, and as she tried to push him away, Raziel gripped her wrists firmly. She could taste liquor on his breath. "Christ, I've been thinking about your legs wrapped around me all day," he growled as he pushed up her skirt.

"Raz, stop." Winter was breathless, but he didn't listen to her. Winter gave in, suddenly afraid of what he might do if she tried to escape him. He took her there, in her small galley kitchen, kissing her tenderly as they fucked, and Winter tried to enjoy it, even though she didn't want to make love.

Afterwards, Raziel was loving, leading her back to her bedroom and asking her to lay down with him. He trailed a finger down her cheek. "I'm sorry, but I missed you so much, baby."

She swallowed hard and tried to smile. Raziel clearly didn't want to hear what she had to say. *Fine,* she thought, *I'll humor you a little while longer.*

Raziel unbuttoned her shirt and kissed her exposed skin, pulling down the lacy cup of her bra to take her nipple into his mouth. Winter tried to relax, but when she closed her eyes, almost immediately, unbidden came the fantasy that it was Satchel Rose whose tongue flicked around her nipple so hungrily. That it was his hand that stroked her belly and slipped between her legs to caress her sex. She gave a little moan and felt the pressure increase. Soon, Raziel was inside her again, his lips against hers, and yet all Winter could think about was how it would feel to have Satchel Rose holding her. Picturing his face sent a raging fire through her veins, and she came hard, moaning, arching her back up.

As she caught her breath, she pushed her fantasy away and braced herself as she opened her eyes. Raziel smiled down at her. "You have to admit, beautiful. We're damn good when we're together like this."

She nodded, hoping the guilt wasn't obvious in her eyes. She buried her face in his chest and tried not let the overwhelming longing she felt consume her.

Raziel stroked her hair. "My darling Winter... I think we both know this is more than just a casual thing." He slid his hand under her chin and made her look up at him. "I'm not a man who easily relinquishes what he wants, Winter."

Winter swallowed. "Raziel... I meant what I said. I'm not looking for a relationship."

"And yet here we are, clearly at the start of one." Raziel sat up, keeping his arms around her. It felt like a cage. "I'm offering you the world, Winter. Anything your heart could desire."

She shook her head. "I'm not looking for riches or a life of luxury. I'm happy as I am."

Raziel looked around her threadbare but comfortable home, and a small smirk appeared at the corner of his mouth. "Right."

Winter flushed. *Asshole.* She extracted herself from his arms and grabbed her robe. "I have to get back to what I was doing."

"Of course." Raziel got up and dressed himself, smiling at her, and although she was annoyed, Winter couldn't see any malice in his eyes. "Winter, I'm just saying, I'd like to see where this goes and maybe we could spend more time together. My business practically runs itself. We could do more than just fuck each other. We could go to dinner again, have coffee, peruse bookstores together."

A jolt of shock went through her at his words. "What?"

"I thought you liked bookstores." It was said in all innocence, but Winter had gone cold. Was that a snipe at her for meeting Satchel? Was he having her followed?

Winter shrugged. "Let's just take things slowly."

"Of course." He kissed her cheek, all business now, as he tugged on his pants. Winter left him to dress and went out to unpack her groceries. As Raz entered, he picked up the paper. Winter saw him reading the headline.

"She disappeared from around here," she said lightly. "What's funny is, the night she disappeared, I heard a scream. I thought I had dreamed it, but others heard it to. Did you?"

Raziel shook his head, his expression blank. "No, but with respect, my yacht has, shall we say, better insulation against the outside."

Winter flushed at the jibe, feeling defensive of her raggedy home. It was hers. She shrugged off his comment and left the subject alone. Raz put his hand on the back of her neck and leaned in for a kiss. "Happy Thanksgiving, beautiful. If you change your mind about tomorrow night, you're always welcome to come to the yacht."

"Thank you."

WINTER HEAVED a sigh of relief when he'd gone and then felt guilty. Maybe it was guilt over her feelings for Satchel Rose—a stupid crush, she told herself. I mean how much could I know about the man after two short meetings? Or maybe it was that Raziel exuded power and dominance, so much so that she felt... *inferior* wasn't the word, but... somehow, she felt as if she were one of the staff rather than an equal, someone he could fuck when he felt like it, someone he could parade on his arm when he needed it. With Raziel Ganz, she knew, deep in her bones, she would never have her own agency.

She shook her head. *No. Get Thanksgiving out of the way, then tell him it is over.* It wasn't fair to either of them to continue whatever this was.

It was over.

CHAPTER THIRTEEN

J anelle fixed her stepson with a beady eye. "You've been quiet this whole day. Not moody, just quiet. What's up?"

Satchel grinned at her. "I'm just overdosed on your incredible food."

Janelle snorted. "Yeah, yeah, try to distract me, but you have something on your mind. Come on. Your pa's asleep and I won't tell."

They both looked over at the sleeping figure of Patrick, snoring gently in his favorite armchair and Satchel laughed. "I see my future and it looks... relaxing."

"Hmmph. You need a woman in your life. Oh..." Janelle's eyes searched his. "I saw that little flicker in your eyes. You met someone?"

Satchel sighed. He hadn't talked to anyone about Winter Mai yet, and he was almost desperate to. Janelle had been at his side in the aftermath of the shooting and knew who the Mai girls were. He sucked in a calming breath. "Winter Mai."

Janelle's eyes widened, and she shook her head. "Oh, no, Satchel. That's not a good idea."

"I know, Jan, but I can't stop thinking about her." He sighed. "We met by accident twice. The second time we talked, and I mean *talked*, and I knew then I had to see her again."

"Darling," Janelle sat down next to him and took his hand. "Your guilt over Callan... This is not a good idea. That little girl is already damaged." She patted his hand and looked over at Patrick. "Your dad told me he saw you sitting with her in the hospital. Does she know that?"

Satchel shook his head. "There's something between us, Janelle. I can't tell you what, or if anything will happen, but I know there's... something."

Janelle sighed and passed her hand over her eyes. Satchel waited, but both were surprised when Patrick spoke. "That girl's been through enough, son. If you go for it, you make absolutely sure she— and you—know what you're getting into. But Janelle's right. This is a bad idea."

Satchel slumped back in his seat, feeling like a sulky teenager. Were they right? Maybe, but they hadn't sensed the incredible connection that had passed between he and Winter. Maybe in some twisted, fucked-up way, they had been destined to meet.

Jesus, you sound like a Hallmark card. Satchel changed the subject, and the rest of the evening passed off pleasantly enough.

At eight, he went into the hallway and picked up the phone to make the call he had made every year since he was a kid. This time though, and for the last three years, he only spoken to Callan's parents and not Callan himself.

Callan's father, Hamish, a Scottish immigrant, spoke to him briefly and wished him a happy Thanksgiving. "Damn ungrateful Colonial."

Satchel chuckled. Hamish made the same joke every year despite the fact he himself had spent more of his life in the United States than in his native Scotland. His wife, Callan's mother, Ricki Lee, took the phone then and said hello. She sounded like she had been crying.

"You okay, Ricki?"

Ricki sighed. "Just missing my boy, Satchie. He told us he didn't want us to visit this year."

"I'm sorry, Ricki. You should have come to Portland and spent it with us."

Ricki gave a short laugh. "You are a sweet boy, Satchie."

Satchel talked with them both for a few more minutes, then hung up. He walked to the large window of his dad's mansion and looked out over Portland. His father's house was built high on a hillside overlooking the city, and Satchel had always loved this view. Suddenly he pictured standing here with Winter, his arms around her, his lips against her temple. God, was he being stupid? What could he possibly know from two very brief conversations and those nights holding her hand as she lay unconscious?

No. The best he could do for her, the only thing he was entitled to do, was keep his meeting with Raziel, become his buddy, look out for Winter that way.

Satchel went to his room and grabbed his cell phone. Agent Holbrook had told him to call him at any time, and even thought it was late on Thanksgiving night, Satchel need to talk to him.

Holbrook answered on the first ring. "Hey, Satchel, Happy Thanksgiving."

"Hello, Agent Holbrook. I'm sorry to disturb your family time."

Holbrook gave a short laugh. "I'm a lifelong bachelor, Satchel. I volunteered for duty tonight, so this is no problem. What's up?"

Satchel told him he had met with Raziel Ganz, and that he had also learned that Winter Mai was involved with him. "She's someone I care about, Agent Holbrook. I'm concerned for her safety."

Holbrook sighed. "I know. Listen, you're not going to want to hear this, Satchel, but this is bigger than just one woman. Dozens, maybe even hundreds of young women and children are being trafficked, and, we suspect, murdered by Ganz and his partners."

"Why is it you suspect him but have no evidence?"

Holbrook sighed. "Because our informers end up dead. We think Ganz has friends in the upper echelons of police, government... why do you think he wants to get to your father?"

Satchel felt a tight fist in his chest. "I won't let him fool my dad into helping him. I can run interference for a while."

"Good, do that. But befriend the guy. Any information will be helpful. And maybe, just maybe, I can look into getting your friend, Winter, some protection."

Satchel had to be satisfied with that, but later, as he lay in bed, he swore to himself he would protect Winter Mai from Raziel Ganz. She obviously had no idea what he was capable of.

This is bigger than just one woman...

"No," he said to himself now, "it's not..."

THE TENSION in Winter's body seemed to spill away as she spent the afternoon and evening with Joe and Cassie. The young couple were relentlessly loving and upbeat, and Winter's mood lifted as they ate Cassie's delicious food and played board games, drinking beer and listening to music.

Cassie flopped down on the sofa beside Winter as Joe went to replenish their drinks. "Sure you don't want to stay the night? This sofa pulls out."

"You're very kind," Winter said, smiling at her friend, "but I have a student first thing in the morning."

"At least stay until after the fireworks have finished. I know you hate them." Cassie patted Winter's leg, and Winter felt a rush of love for her friend.

"You and Joe... you've been like family to me," she said, her voice breaking slightly, her emotions close to the surface.

"Mushy..." teased Cassie as Joe returned, and they both ribbed Winter until she was giggling helplessly.

"You guys kill me."

Laughing with them, Winter felt more like her old self, remembering when she, Summer, and Autumn used to fool around and tease each other. It had always been Summer and Winter ganging up on their older sister. Autumn, always the thickest skinned of the Mai girls, had taken it in good humor and held her own in the games they played.

God, it seemed so long ago. Winter hardly remembered what it felt like to be part of a family. Maybe she should call... she checked her watch. It was eleven p.m. in Portland; it was far too late in New York to call now. She felt sadness in her chest. Maybe it was time to rebuild what had been lost.

Winter took a cab back to her home, relived that she had missed the fireworks. The harbor was quiet in the cold night and she saw, happily, that Raziel's yacht was in darkness.

She went into her home and shut the door behind her, but a few seconds later, she heard a knock. She sighed; there was no doubt who her visitor would be. Should she ignore him? She had yet to turn the lights on, but he undoubtedly had been watching for her to come home.

God. What had she got herself into?

She went to the door. Raz smiled at her. "Happy Thanksgiving, darling."

Be nice. "Happy Thanksgiving, Raziel."

He smiled, his eyes soft. "May I come in?"

She stepped back to let him in. "You look beautiful."

She looked down at her old navy sweater and jeans. "In this?"

Raziel laughed. "You always look beautiful. Come here to me."

Ah, screw it. She was drunk, and it was nice to be held by a man. It was just... why couldn't it be Satchel Rose?

She pushed that thought away and went into Raziel's open arms. The alcohol had made her fuzzy and pliable, and soon she found herself naked as Raziel pushed her legs apart and took her clit into his mouth. His hands were on her hips, fingers digging into the soft flesh, holding her tightly.

Winter closed her eyes and let him make love to her, her senses whirling with endorphins. She moaned as he brought her near to orgasm, and then as she tipped over into ecstasy, she cried out.

Suddenly the pressure on her clit stopped. "What the hell did you just say?"

Winter's eyes popped open. What? What had she said? "What do you mean?"

Raziel was sitting on the edge of the bed now, his head in his hands. "Jesus."

Winter felt panic... what had she said? "I don't understand... what did I say?"

Raziel looked over at her, and she was shocked at the heartbreak in his eyes. "You said his name."

"Whose name?"

Raziel took a deep breath. "You said... *Oh, Satchel...*"

"No. No, I did *not*. Why would I?"

"You tell me."

Winter put a tentative hand on Raziel's shoulder. "You misheard... darling." Ugh, she hated calling him that, but she did feel sorry for him. "I'm making love with *you*, Raziel... Raziel, Satchel... they don't sound dissimilar. I wouldn't say another man's name, I swear." *Even if I am drunk, and I wish it* were *Satchel Rose in this bed with me...*

God, she disgusted herself. Was this what she had become? A cheater, not physically, but emotionally? "I'm sorry, baby." This time, she meant her apology, and she wrapped her arms around him. "I swear, this is you and me."

He was stone faced for a moment, then he relaxed, and she pulled him back down to the bed, laying on top of him. He took her face in his hands, his eyes raking hers. Winter winced as his fingers tangled in her hair, pulling it. "I don't share," he said softly, and Winter nodded.

"Raziel, when it's the two of us, it's just the two of us."

The pressure tightened for a moment, almost painfully, then released, and he pulled her lips to his, and Winter pushed all thoughts of Satchel to the back of her head. She wasn't a cheater, no way, and while she was sleeping with this man, then she was with him—Raziel.

She tried to dismiss the fear that had crept into her soul when she saw the hurt—and anger—in his eyes... the violence.

For now, he was tender, loving, affectionate, and she focused just on that for tonight. He fell asleep in her arms, and Winter resolved, when she was sober, to talk with him, tell him that they should just be friends. She owed him that much.

When she woke in the morning, he was gone. Winter sighed with relief. Today she would start to sort this damn mess out and move on with her life. She swung her legs over the side of the bed and stopped.

On the nightstand was a tidy stack of hundred-dollar bills and a note.

Thank you for a wonderful night...

CHAPTER FOURTEEN

S atchel waited for Raziel to be ready to meet with him. He glanced over at the assistant who had greeted him, and the man nodded. "I'm sorry, Mr. Rose. He's just stuck on a call."

"It's no problem, really." Satchel got up and casually strolled around the deck. His eyes lit on the small houseboat next to the yacht. A smile crept across his face. Winter. The little place suited her, and now as he listened, he could hear her piano faintly.

"Satchel, I'm sorry to have kept you waiting."

Satchel turned to see Raziel Ganz smiling at him, his hand outstretched to greet him. He shook it. "Come back to my office, as it is. I haven't found suitable premises in the city for my headquarters as yet... maybe you could suggest somewhere?"

"Of course," Satchel said smoothly as he followed Raziel inside. "There are a few good options I can think of just off the top of my head."

Raz led him to his office and offered him a seat. "That's what I wanted to hear."

Satchel nodded. "Listen, I'm sure I'm not just here because you want to know the best real estate in the city."

"You're a straight shooter."

"I try to be." Satchel met his steady gaze. "I'm guessing this is more about who my father is than me."

Raz smiled. "Listen, it's about you both. Yes, having your father as a trusted ally on the board of the city would be advantageous. But I also have another project in mind, and you're definitely the guy in Portland for it."

"And that is?"

Raz opened a drawer in his desk and pulled put a file, handing it to Satchel. Satchel opened it and read through the first page. His heart began to beat a little faster. "Homeless shelters?"

"I made a lot of money very fast. Now it's time to give something back."

"I see." Satchel read through some more of the paperwork. Homeless shelters? A never-ending stream of people desperate for help—and ripe for selling? Fuck... "Have you talked to the established charities in Portland? Transition Projects? The Human Solutions Family Center?"

"Of course. We've been in discussion with them for a few months now. They're on board, of course, but we need premises, and that's where you come in." He pulled a blueprint from a shelf next to his desk and spread it out. "Here's the layout we've been thinking of. We want to provide the basics: food, heat, beds, and hot water, but we also want to mentor them, help them get jobs, homes, the whole works. Get them off welfare."

"Hmm." He had to admit, Ganz sounded genuine, but as Satchel studied the plans, he was looking at all the ways people could be processed through these buildings—and never be seen again. "So, what is it you want from me? You have the blueprints, the designs already."

"A partner. Someone who is respected in the Portland community." Raziel smiled. "And yes, who has influence with the City. I won't deny your father could be very useful to this project and with... any future political plans I might have."

Satchel kept his expression neutral. If he wasn't already aware of the FBI's suspicions, he could quite easily buy Raziel Ganz's charm offensive. The man was intelligent, erudite... and utterly corrupt. The thought of his hands on Winter made Satchel want to throw up.

Focus. "Look, we can certainly talk about this more. Let's have dinner. Bring Winter and I'll... bring a date." God, any excuse to see them together, to see what there was between them. To know she at least was safe for a few hours.

Raz's eyes took on an unknowable look. "Good idea. I'll ask Gareth to call your assistant."

"Fine. Look, as my father, I have to tell you... we work hard not to be seen as colluding—I never go to him for permits or the like, but I can effect an introduction. After that, it's up to you."

"I appreciate it."

As HE LEFT, Satchel had to stop himself from calling at Winter's houseboat. As he strode past on the jetty, he shot a glance through the window and saw her laughing with a student who was sitting at a piano. God, to see her smile...

He got into his car and drove back to his own office. Shutting the door, he placed a call to Agent Holbrook and relayed what had happened at the meeting.

Guy Holbrook hissed between his teeth. "Well, he's trying to hide in plain sight, isn't he? Damn, he's arrogant."

"To say the least."

Holbrook thanked Satchel and ended the call. Satchel sat at his desk, wondering what the hell to do next. Finding premises for Ganz, to at least looking like he was trying would be a start, but Satchel resented the time he would waste on this.

If it keeps Ganz happy and Winter safe...

His cell phone buzzed, and he glanced at the display before grinning. He picked up. "Mallory. I'm sorry I haven't called back."

"No biggie, Rose, buddy, but I just wanted to check you wanted me to continue this story. I've been doing some digging about your girl Winter, and she's a pretty closed book. I contacted her family in New York, her sister the chef, but got nowhere. Autumn Mai told me in no certain terms that Winter was off limits." Mallory sighed. "I'm sorry, pal, but there doesn't seem to be a story there."

Satchel sighed. "Well, you tried. I appreciate it." He tapped his pencil on his desk, thinking. "What about a new scheme for the homeless in the city? A partnership between Rose Property and Ganz, Inc? We're in preliminary discussions." He mentally crossed his fingers that Holbrook would be okay with this, but if Mallory could get out that Winter was with Ganz, it would make it harder for Ganz to make her disappear—if indeed that was his plan for her. For all he knew, Ganz could be head over heels for Winter. Satchel could understand that.

Mallory considered. "Can you get me in with Ganz, one-to-one?"

"I can certainly ask. He wants favors from me; this could be *quid pro quo*. Clarice," he added as she laughed at his repeating of her line back at him. "I'll get back to you, Mal."

"Be sure you do, handsome."

Satchel ended the call smiling. If he could go all out protecting Winter from Ganz—*and, let's face it, Rose, you have no rights here*—then he could box Ganz into a corner. Keep Winter front and center.

Satisfied, Satchel called Molly into his office and got to work.

WINTER HAD KEPT her anger bottled while she worked with her first student of the day and even gave a great performance of being happy and lighthearted.

But inside she was raging. Money on the nightstand. Could there be any more offensive thing he could do? Like she was some cheap *whore. Thanks for the great sex, here's your reward.*

She'd underestimated how pissed he was at her slip of the tongue —if indeed she *had* said Satchel's name out loud—but this was beyond insulting.

When her student left, Winter steeled herself and let her rage bubble up. She grabbed the stack of money—and there were a couple thousand bucks there—and stomped up to the yacht. She didn't even say hello to Davide as he stepped aside to let her in.

Winter's anger was white hot as she reached the deck and saw Raz reclining back on a chair, drink in hand. His eyes were cold, but he smiled as she approached and didn't even flinch as she threw the money in his face. "What the fuck is this?"

He waited until the money had fluttered to the shipboards, peeled a stray note from his shirt, and dropped it on the deck casually. "I thought you were broke."

"What the fuck do you know about my finances?"

She clenched her hands into fists as he slowly looked her up and down and then over to her ramshackle home. "I have eyes, Winter."

"You bastard!" Her hand whipped out, and she slapped him solidly. She barely had time before Raziel was up, grasping her wrists, forcing her back against the wall of the cabin.

"You *never* hit me, little girl, do you understand?" He yanked her back toward him and then slammed her hard again. His face was a mask of utter rage: red, puffy, contorted with anger. Winter ripped her wrists away from him. He had made this easier for her, and she wasn't afraid of him.

"Stay away from me, asshole. This is *over*."

SHE EXPECTED him to follow her but was relieved when he didn't. She went to the harbor master and asked him how much it would cost to relocate her houseboat away from the yacht. The man took pity on her, seeing her distress. "Listen, Mason Harris is looking for a new spot. What say we do a straight swap and it won't cost you a penny?"

Winter felt weak with relief. "God, thank you."

The only downside was that it would take a week to move, but she would take what she could get. Maybe she should sell the houseboat and get a small apartment in the city. She could get a part-time job, even if that meant interacting with more people, but hell, maybe it was time. She was too isolated.

Winter didn't go home right away, instead she walked into the city. As she walked, she wished she had some way to contact Satchel Rose.

What are you thinking? You really need another complication?

No. She was meeting him at the bookstore in a couple of days anyway. Besides, there was a phone call she needed to make to someone that was way, way overdue. She walked to a coffeehouse and sat down at a table, taking out her phone. There was no reason she should be in this alone...

"Auttie? It's me."

There was silence on the other end of the line. Then she heard her sister clear her throat. "Hello, Winter."

Her tone wasn't exactly warm, but Winter didn't blame her. "I just wanted to... say Happy Thanksgiving."

At first, she thought Autumn was laughing, then she realized her sister was crying. "Auttie..."

"Happy Thanksgiving? Helga *died*, Winter. She died. I went to bring her tea in the morning and she was just gone."

Winter felt the shock like a sledgehammer. "Oh, God, Auttie..."

"I tried to revive her, but she was long gone. Just like that. Quiet. Peaceful. And final."

Winter felt hot tears pour down her face. "Auttie... Look, I'll come. I'll get on a bus and come to the funeral and..."

"Don't bother," her sister spat out, finally. "You haven't given a flying fuck about us for three years. Why bother now? I don't want you there."

The line went dead, and Winter dropped it with a clatter on the table. Like a zombie she got up and walked out of the coffee house, barely registering the barista chasing and calling after her. "Miss, you dropped your phone."

She stared at him blankly as he handed her the phone, and he blinked, looking slightly alarmed. "Hey, are you okay?"

She shook her head. "No... but thank you."

"I can call someone for you."

She tried to smile. "There's no one to call," she whispered and began to walk away from him.

Winter walked for miles until it began to get dark. It was late November, and the weather was bitingly cold, and her coat was thin.

Somehow, she made it home and went inside locking the door behind her, leaving the lights off.

Fully clothed, she curled up on her bed, too numb to cry now. Helga, her beloved aunt, the woman who had raised her and her sisters was gone, and because of her own damn stubbornness, she hadn't been able to say goodbye. Autumn, her last remaining family had made it clear: Winter had wanted to be alone and now she had her wish.

Winter closed her eyes. Right now, if she didn't wake up in the morning, that would be okay. She was alone, with a rich man for an enemy, and a sister who hated her.

Somehow, exhausted, she fell asleep only to be woken by the urgent need to vomit only a few hours later. She dashed to the toilet and threw up again and again until she was dry-heaving and sobbing. Stomach flu was all she needed right now...

She curled up on the cool tile of the bathroom floor, a feat in itself in the tiny room, but the cold tile against her hot skin was comforting. She felt asleep again, dozing restlessly...

Pop-pop-pop-pop-pop-pop-pop...

Her eyes flew open as she heard the gunfire... fireworks? The sky was lit up, but she could swear it wasn't just fireworks...

She blocked her ears, a keening, desiccating scream coming from her already raw throat. The madness was settling in, as she tried to block out the noise, the chaos.

It seemed to go on for hours, but when she smelled smoke, Winter had to fight to take control of her senses. She reached over to the living room door, but as she touched the knob, she recoiled. It was burning hot. Smoke pumped under the door.

The houseboat was on fire.

Winter skittered backwards in the tight space. She was trapped. There were windows in the bedroom and bathroom, but both were tiny, not even big enough to fit her petite body through.

Winter began to cough as smoke filled the room, and for one moment, she thought about giving into it, just letting go...

"Winter!"

She heard a male voice screaming her name as she began to lose consciousness and heard the door to her bedroom being kicked in. She wanted to scream that the fire would get in, that whoever it was should leave her, but then she felt herself being lifted, carried out of the burning houseboat.

Sirens. There were sirens now, and people shouting. Fresh air. Winter was locked in her rescuer's arms, and now as she heard his voice, she knew it was Raziel. He sounded panicked as he begged them to save her. An oxygen mask was placed over her head and a woman with a kind face came into her vision. "Hey, sweetheart, can you tell me your name?"

Winter mumbled her name, but by the look on the woman's face, she wasn't making any sense. "Okay, sweetie, just breathe deep, we're going to get you to the emergency room."

The paramedic looked up and addressed Raziel. "Sir, are you with this young lady?"

Winter didn't hear his response, but he must have said yes because the woman began to ask him questions. *Does she have a family, any allergies, any medications......* Winter drifted. It was hard to breathe even with the oxygen mask and for now, she didn't care. She wanted oblivion; she wanted peace. So with a sigh, Winter finally let herself go dark.

CHAPTER FIFTEEN

S atchel didn't learn about the fire right away. He was at a site outside the city for most of the morning, but then as he drove home, he switched the radio on and heard about it.

"City fire chiefs say that as many as fifteen vessels and residences at the harbor were destroyed in the fire, but as yet the injury count is unknown. There have been no fatalities reported yet, but a number of residents were taken to the emergency room, suffering from burns and smoke inhalation. The cause of the devastating fire is yet unknown."

Satchel turned the car around with a skid, invoking honking car horns from other drivers, and he sped down to the harbor. He could only get so close with the car, so he hurriedly parked and walked down the jetty. He could see Ganz's yacht, unharmed by the fire, but the smoking remains of Winter's houseboat took his breath away. God, was she okay?

He managed to slip past the police and fire officers and walked quickly to Ganz's yacht. Ganz's security guard nodded to him. "Mr. Rose."

"Hey... is Mr. Ganz here? Is he okay?"

Davide nodded. "He's fine, thank you, Mr. Rose. He's at the hospital with his fiancée."

Satchel felt like a wrecking ball had hit his chest. "His fiancée?"

"Miss Mai. She was in her houseboat when it caught fire. Mr. Ganz pulled her out, and they took her to the emergency room."

"Is she okay?"

"I don't have any other news, I'm sorry."

Satchel stared at him, knowing the horror was showing on his face. "Which hospital?"

Davide told him, and mumbling his thanks, Satchel stumbled back to his car. Winter was hurt... and *engaged. No. No way.* That must a mistake... but a small voice in his head was telling him not to presume, that he didn't really know her after all. That she might well have said yes to Ganz, the powerful, rich man who could take care of her.

Her savior, after all. Regardless of anything else, Satchel knew he should feel grateful that Ganz saved Winter's life.

Focus on that for now. Just focus on that.

He was walking through the hospital corridors before he knew it and stopped only as he reached the emergency room. What was he going to say? Would his presence cause more trouble for Winter? Would Ganz question why he was there?

Fuck it. He needed to know Winter was okay. Satchel pushed into the emergency room area and looked around. A nurse approached him, and he asked where Mr. Ganz was. The nurse told him, and Satchel followed her directions to a private room.

He knocked. After a moment the door opened, and Raziel Ganz came out. He looked shocked to see Satchel. "Rose? What are you doing here?"

"I heard about the fire. Are you okay? I thought, as you don't know many people in the city, I'd come and check."

Raziel's lips twitched, a half-smile on his mouth. Mocking. He knew exactly why Satchel was there—and knew it wasn't for him. "I'm fine. That's very kind of you, Rose. I'm not used to my business contacts caring about my well-being."

Satchel knew he was busted but didn't care. "I saw the damage at the harbor and your security man told me Miss Mai was hurt."

Raziel closed the door behind him. "Smoke inhalation. She's being treated, but she should be fine. Thank you for your concern. I'll pass along your best wishes."

It was obvious Ganz wasn't about to let Satchel see Winter, and Satchel could do nothing about it. If it was true Ganz was engaged to Winter, he was her next of kin. "Can I do anything to help you? Maybe contact Miss Mai's family?"

Again, that mocking smile. "It's all in hand, thank you."

Dismissal. Satchel nodded and turned on his heel.

"Rose."

He turned back to see Ganz smiling at him. "I won't forget your... concern."

Asshole. "My best wishes to Miss Mai."

"I'll let her know."

Sure you will... Satchel stalked out of the hospital and back to his car. He sat for a while, letting his anger dissipate. *What did you expect? You're projecting a relationship with Winter that doesn't exist except in your fantasies. She's with Ganz. That's it. Deal with it.*

"Fuck!" Satchel beat the steering wheel for a moment, then stopped as he'd attracted the attention of some passersby. Great. That's all he needed, to be caught freaking out in a hospital parking lot. He rubbed his face. Was he losing it? Was this some residue kick-back from the horror of Callan and the massacre? Guilt mixed with the desperate need to make amends?

Satchel glanced at his reflection in the rearview mirror. His eyes were almost wild. "Jesus, you are losing it, buddy."

He shook his head as he steered the car out of the lot and towards home. Halfway there, he had an idea and went into the city instead. If Ganz wasn't going to let him see Winter, then he would have to find another way of contacting her, of telling her he was there if she needed help. He could only offer—Winter would be the one to decide whether to get in touch.

And then... he would know.

· · ·

WINTER WOKE to a coughing fit and a nurse holding a paper bowl under her chin to catch the dirty, black sputum she was bringing up.

"That's it, sweetie. That's the best thing you can do; get that muck out of your system." The nurse was rubbing her back as Winter almost choked, desperate for oxygen. She sat back, gasping as the nurse fixed the oxygen mask back over her face and took her vitals.

The nurse, a kind-faced woman named Vera, smiled at her. "Your handsome fiancé is waiting just outside."

Winter closed her eyes. *Fiancé.* She hadn't had the strength to tell anyone Raziel wasn't her fiancé, but the thought made her gag, even if he *had* been the one to save her life.

There was a deep, utterly profound certainty inside of her that Raziel was the reason she was in a hospital in the first place.

But now she had nothing, not even the underwear she had been wearing in bed. Her home was gone, her clothes, her beloved piano, everything. She literally had *nothing. I don't even own a toothbrush,* she thought now and started to cry.

"Hey, hey, hey..." Vera put her arm around the sobbing girl. "It's okay, sweetie."

It isn't. None of this is okay. How the hell was she was supposed to find the money to pay her hospital bills?

Raziel came into the room, and Vera smiled at him. "Look who is here, lovely." She got off the side of the bed, nodding at Raz, who sat in her place, locking his arms around Winter. "I'll leave you two love-birds alone."

No, don't go... but Vera shut the door behind her, and she was alone with Raziel. His lips were against her temple. "Oh, darling, when I saw your boat on fire... I could have lost you forever."

He sounded so genuine that Winter could almost believe him. She pulled away slightly and gazed up at him. His eyes were soft and loving, the opposite of the raging, violent man she had last seen. He nodded, as if reading her thoughts. "Darling, I'm so sorry about how I behaved yesterday. I was an absolute bastard. I have no excuse except I was upset that you said... never mind."

Winter said nothing, looking away from him. *I have nothing. No one. And he knows it.*

"I want you to know that everything is being taken care of: the medical bills, the clean-up of the boat... everything."

And he knows I'm in debt to him. Jesus. I'll never get away from him now. She felt herself gag, and Raz got up in alarm, grabbing the bowl she had spit up in earlier. "Here, baby."

To his credit, he held her hair back while she threw up, vomit mixed with the black phlegm now. "Christ, Winter, maybe I'd better get the nurse."

"No," her voice was gravelly as she leaned back against the pillows. "I'm okay."

Raziel went to the bathroom and fetched a damp towelette for her. "Here."

She murmured her thanks as she wiped her mouth, which tasted foul. She didn't care. *Try to kiss me now, asshole.* "Did you call my family?"

Raz nodded, sweeping a cool hand over her hot forehead. "I did, sweetheart. Your sister said... God, Winter, I'm so sorry..."

Winter closed her eyes. Autumn really was done with her. "It's okay."

"That's why I had to tell them we were engaged, otherwise they wouldn't have told me anything."

"Fine." God, what did it matter now? It was hopeless.

"Your home... there's nothing left, darling, but I don't want you to worry. You'll come live with me until we can get you back on your feet." He gave her a crooked smile. "But maybe by then, you won't want your own place again." He picked up her fingers and kissed the tops of them. "When I thought I'd lost you, Winter, I knew. I knew I was in love with you."

Winter felt sick again. "You don't even know me," she whispered, and Raz smiled.

"But I do, darling, more than you know. But, listen, just rest now. We have all the time in the world to talk about our future."

He kissed her forehead. "I have to go take care of some business, darling. I'll be back later."

WHEN SHE WAS ALONE, Winter shuffled out of bed and went to the bathroom. She could barely stand to see herself in the mirror, her olive skin was wan and her hair lank and stinking of smoke. She peeled the hospital gown off and stepped into the shower, shampooing her hair and trying not to cough too much, worried she would throw up.

The shower made her feel infinitely better, at least physically, and she grabbed a fresh gown from behind the door, wrapping it tightly around her body. Another wave of nausea hit her, and she threw up again, half-sobbing. Her stomach was cramping badly, and she knew she had to confront the fact that maybe, just maybe, there was yet another problem to contend with.

One that if true, Raziel would use to hold over her head for the rest of her life.

No. It was time to find out if it was true or not. She took some deep breaths and then brushed her teeth. As she finished, there was a knock at the door, and a tall woman in a white coat came into the room.

"Hi, Winter, I'm Dr. Fleming, I've been treating you since you came in. Why don't you sit back on the bed so I can check you out?"

As the doctor examined her, Winter tried to figure out whether she was an ally or not. Stop being paranoid. "Doc?"

"Yes, hon?"

Winter bit her lip before continuing. "Does a pregnancy test show up on a medical bill?"

The doctor stopped what she was doing and studied Winter. "Do you think you're pregnant, sweetie?"

"I might be."

"And you don't want your fiancé to know about it?"

Winter took a deep breath. "He's *not* my fiancé, but he's insisting on paying for everything and I... if he sees a pregnancy test on the medical bill..."

The doctor nodded, her eyes full of understanding. "I can do the test without putting your name on it. Honey... do you need help?"

Winter half-laughed, half-sobbed. "I just need to know how fucked I am."

Dr. Fleming perched on the side of the bed. "Winter..."

"For now. Just the test, please. Then I'll know what to do."

She could see the doctor wasn't happy, but she took the blood sample anyway. "I'll put a rush on it, honey. Just between you and me."

"Thank you so much." Winter's eyes filled with tears. Damn it, was she so depressed any kindness felt like a victory, now?

The doctor squeezed her shoulder. "I'll be back as soon as I can. Winter... would you like me to put a 'Do Not Disturb' sign on your door? I can keep visitors out... *all* visitors?"

Winter nodded.

"Consider it done," the doctor winked at her, and Winter knew she had found a friend.

Peace. For the first time, she felt as if she were doing something positive—facing the truth, whatever it was, head on. Once she knew, she could make plans...

"Ha. Make plans with what?" She was utterly destitute. Maybe she could ask Joe and Cassie if she could sleep on their couch while she tried to sort her fucked-up life out. She knew they would say yes, but God, she hated to impose.

There is someone else you could ask...

No. She would not drag Satchel Rose into this; the man owed her nothing and, Christ, they had spoken only twice in her life. Twice!

But the thought of his arms around her now, her head resting against his chest, his warm voice reassuring her everything would be okay... It was okay to cling to that fantasy now, right? Just for comfort? As long as she didn't believe it could be real, what harm could it do?

. . .

BUT THEN, an hour later, she knew that the fantasy would only ever be that. She couldn't ask Satchel for help, couldn't go to anyone else for help. She was trapped.

Because she was pregnant with Raziel Ganz's child.

CHAPTER SIXTEEN

Molly Hammond spoke to reception and was directed to the floor where Winter was recovering. When she got there, however, she was told that Winter was not receiving visitors under any circumstances.

"I'm sorry, ma'am. Miss Mai doesn't want to see anyone."

Molly nodded. "That's fine, but perhaps you could give her these flowers? They're from a friend."

"I'm sure we can—" The nurse stopped as they both heard a man's raised voice.

"I'm her fucking *fiancé*, and you're telling me I can't go in?"

Molly watched as a tall, handsome man in an expensive suit ranted at an unimpressed female doctor. Surreptitiously, Molly began to record the confrontation on her phone. *Information.* That what Satchel had sent her for, and this was gold. Molly recognized Raziel Ganz from Satchel's description.

"Mr. Ganz," the doctor was saying to him, "We have to think of Miss Mai's recovery. She needs rest. I'm sure as soon as she feels up to it, she'll see you."

Molly watched as Ganz's face grew redder, and she held her

breath. He looked like he wanted to hit the doctor, who stood her ground with her eyes narrowed. Finally, Ganz walked off, cursing to himself, barking orders at the goon squad that he had brought with him.

The doctor let out a long breath and came to the nurse's station. "Asshole," she muttered, and Molly snorted. The doctor grinned at her. "You didn't hear that, okay?"

"Hear what?"

"Good girl. Those for a patient?"

"For Winter Mai. It's okay, I know she doesn't want visitors but if someone could give these to her?"

"No, problem."

Molly thanked the doctor and nurse and returned to her car. As she sat, she saw Ganz and his cronies walking across the lot and instinctively locked her car doors. There was something so... *sinister* about the man. Molly shivered and called Satchel.

"Hey, Mols. It's done?"

"It is, but get this..." She told Satchel about the confrontation between Ganz and the doctor. "It sounds like Winter's banned him from visiting her... He was screaming that she was his fiancée which gave him the right to supercede her wishes. He didn't get his way."

"Remind me to send her doctor a bouquet, too," Satchel said grimly, then sighed. "Molly... do you think I'm overstepping?"

"All you've done so far is send flowers... and a burner phone. And that's if she finds it. All you've done is give her a way to communicate —and not even necessarily with you. No, Satch, you're not over-stepping."

"Thanks, Mols. Listen, take the rest of the day. You've gone above and beyond."

Molly chuckled. "I won't say no. I have Christmas shopping to do."

WINTER STOOD AT THE WINDOW, watching Raziel and his gang get into their cars and leave the hospital. He'd be mad, but at this moment, she didn't give a crap. Unconsciously she rubbed her hand over her non-existent bump. There was no way she was letting Ganz know she was carrying his child—because it *wasn't* his child. Not in Winter's mind; she and the baby were one, and Winter didn't belong to anyone.

She would find a way to look after both of them; she would find a way to pay back Ganz for every penny of her medical bills, but what she wouldn't do is expose her child to his world. No freakin' way, she said to herself now.

There was a knock at her door and Vera came in, bearing a vast bouquet of roses. "From a friend," she said with a twinkle in her eye. "Damn, this thing is heavy."

Winter helped her place the vase on the nightstand. "They're gorgeous." She breathed in the heavy scent and stroked the velvety petals of the roses. *Roses...* She knew who these were from immediately, and a warm rush flooded her body. "Thank you."

"You're welcome. I'll be back to check your vitals in a little while. Doc says you won't have to be in here much longer, sweetie."

Winter smiled at her, then when she was alone, she looked for a note. There was none, but she didn't need to guess why or who. She lifted the vase to place it closer to her bed—and felt something shift inside the ceramic.

Frowning, she pushed the stems aside and peered into the vase. A bundle was wrapped in plastic and shoved down deep inside the vessel. She fished it out to see a small cell phone. Her heart began to beat as she unwrapped it and switched it on. Only one number was programmed in.

Hope began to blossom in her chest. How did he know? How did Satchel Rose realize what bad news Raziel was? And that she was in trouble?

She quickly shoved the phone underneath her as the door opened, but she was relieved it was only the nurse again, Vera, rolling her eyes. "Your fiancé... sorry, I mean, Mr Ganz is making a fuss to the powers that be again. Honey, your *picker* is broken. I know I shouldn't say that, but—"

Winter laughed. "You're not wrong, Vera. But, look, I don't want to make any trouble." She sat down on the bed. "He can come visit— during visiting hours."

"Whatever you say, honey."

FINALLY, when she was sure she wouldn't be interrupted, she tugged the phone out and dialed the number.

When Satchel said hello, his voice was so warm, so loving that she almost burst into tears. Her fingers were trembling as she thanked him for the flowers and the phone.

"I thought you might need someone to talk to."

"How did you know?" Winter wiped a tear away. "You've thrown me a lifeline, but how? How did you know?"

Satchel hesitated. "I'm not blind, Winter. I saw how unhappy you were."

She did cry then at the tenderness in his voice and at the hopelessness of her situation. "I'm sorry, I didn't mean to cry down the phone at you. I just wanted to hear your voice."

"Me, too. Listen, I want you to keep this phone, and you call me if you need anything. *Anything*, Winter. I can come see you if you want me to."

"I would love to see you, but I don't think that's such a good idea right now."

There was a long silence. "Win?"

She felt warm that he used a nickname for her. "Yes?"

"Did he hurt you?"

She swallowed hard. "He pulled me from the fire."

Another silence. "How did it start?"

It was her turn to be quiet. Could she say the words aloud? "I can't prove anything," she said in the end, feeling lame, but she heard Satchel cuss softly. "Just that day, I had told him it was over between us."

"I see." Satchel sighed. "God. Look, I have some contacts at the police, but for now, just rest and get better. Sweetheart, look. I mean it, you need anything, call me. I owe you."

"No, you don't. You don't, Satchel. I know that now." She closed her eyes. She never wanted to hang up. "But... thank you. At the moment, I have no idea what I'm going to do."

Satchel was quiet again. "Winter... he's telling people you're engaged."

She gave a hollow laugh. "Believe me, that is so far from the truth it's almost funny. Except it's not funny. Nothing about this mess is funny."

"God, I wish..." Satchel broke off, then sighed. "I wish I could say everything I'm feeling right now..."

"Don't." Tears again. "Please, don't. I don't want to wish for a future I can't have."

"Winter..."

"I have to go. Thank you again, Satchel." Winter wanted to scream that she needed him, that she was in trouble, that all she wanted was to be in his arms, but she couldn't. Not now. Now that she was pregnant with Raziel's baby, it wouldn't be fair to Satchel.

"Winter..." Satchel's voice was full of emotion.

"I can't, I'm sorry." She ended the call and burst into tears, crying herself out until a nurse came to give her a sedative.

WHEN SHE WOKE, it was dark outside, and Raziel was in the room with her. "Hello, darling. They say you can go home tomorrow. Isn't that wonderful?"

He kissed her full on the mouth, lingering over the kiss, and when she didn't respond, he drew away, smiling but with his eyes cold. "I've ordered the staff to get our rooms ready for your arrival. One of my assistants has been out shopping for clothes for you; I thought you might appreciate some underwear not provide by the hospital."

Jesus... she didn't even own underwear. Winter closed her eyes. How had everything come to this?

"Winter?"

She opened her eyes. Raziel's gaze was intense on hers. "We will be happy, sweetheart. I know it."

It sounded more like a threat than a promise.

CHAPTER SEVENTEEN

Satchel felt antsy as he sat with Janelle and his father, and he noticed them exchanging worried looks. Finally, his father put his silverware down and cleared his throat.

"What is it, son?"

Satchel drew in a deep breath. "If I tell you something, it can't leave this room."

Janelle squeezed his hand. "You know it won't."

So, he told them about the FBI, about his role in gathering information on Raziel Ganz. "The first time I met the man, I knew. Gut instinct. The guy is a snake." Satchel sighed. "And he's got his hands on Winter. I believe he torched her home, so he could "save" her. I believe he's taken everything from her so that she'll stay with him."

Patrick sighed. "Son... we warned you about that girl."

"She's in trouble, Dad, and goddamn it, I'm... I care for her."

Janelle shook her head. "This won't end well, Satch."

"I won't let him hurt her."

"Satchel. Son." Patrick looked deeply concerned. "Listen to us. You can't interfere. You can't. Unless Winter Mai asks you directly for help, you cannot interfere. The FBI won't thank you for blowing their investigation and more than one life may be forfeit if you do so."

Satchel rubbed his eyes. "You sound like Agent Holbrook. He said that this is bigger than just one woman."

"It is, and you know that." Patrick sighed. "Satchel, your guilt over Callan's act is addling your brain. You don't know this girl. The feelings you have for her are not real. How can they be? You're not a child, but you're acting like a lovesick teenager and messing with things that could cost lives. Do you understand that?"

SATCHEL WENT HOME that night feeling just like a sulky teen, but in his heart, he knew his father was right. He couldn't start a relationship with Winter Mai, but he could still be her friend, right?

Right?

He took his cellphone out. He dared not call her in case Ganz was with her, but he needed to do *something*. He thought about the fact she had no home to go back to now. Maybe he could help there... she had been left with nothing, he guessed, assuming she hadn't been able to afford insurance on her houseboat.

Christ, what must that be like? To have nothing?

He went to bed, his mind whirling with ways to help her, but he couldn't get past the notion that if he helped her, Ganz would react negatively. He needed to keep his distance unless she needed him.

He was just falling asleep when the idea came to him. In the morning, he got up and even before showering he placed a cross-country call to an old friend and colleague in New Orleans. "Arlo? It's Satchel Rose... listen, man, I need a favor..."

WINTER'S CHEST FELT HEAVY, and she couldn't tell whether it was the horror of having to leave the hospital and go home with Raziel, or that she still wasn't well enough. She told Dr. Fleming this, and the doctor understood immediately. She sat on the edge of Winter's bed. "Winter... I can keep you in a few more days if you need more time, but I'm worried. You're obviously scared about going home with Mr. Ganz."

"It's not my home," Winter said, her voice trembling. "I can make other arrangements with some friends in the city, but I wouldn't put it past Raz to sabotage them." Or destroy their lives.

"That is abuse." Fleming said, shaking her head. "Winter, do you think he'll hurt you?"

"Only if I try to leave him, but Dr. Fleming, I'm frightened that he will hurt others if I try to leave the hospital without him. There're also the medical bills. Normally, I would hate that he was paying, but seeing as I believe with all my heart he put me in here, he can pick up the costs. I don't want the hospital to lose out."

"Jesus, Winter, don't worry about that! Your safety is more important. This guy..." The doctor shook her head. "We need to get the police involved."

"No." Winter felt panicky. "No, please. I'll figure something out. Please, this conversation is between us."

"I'm not happy about this."

Winter took a deep breath. "I have to think."

"Well, I'll keep you in for a few days. You tell me what you want to do." Fleming studied her. "Is it the baby?"

She nodded. "I need to figure out what I want."

"Okay. I'll be back later."

WHEN SHE WAS ALONE, Winter stared out of the window, her hand placed on her belly. She knew, in her heart, that she should consider terminating the pregnancy, but something inside her craved this child, no matter who its father was. She felt less alone when she touched her stomach and thought about the little life inside her.

Intellectually, she knew she had nothing with which to support the child, or even herself at the moment, so how the hell was she supposed to bring a child into the world? She shook her head. With Autumn cutting her out of her life, and the only friend she had, Joe and Cassie, not exactly equipped to help her out even if she were to ask—which she wouldn't—there was only one person who could help.

And God, could she really ask Satchel for help while she was carrying another man's baby? Wasn't that cruelty, given the evolving feelings that were passing between them? She would look like such a freaking golddigger, but her situation was dire.

Be honest with Satchel. Tell him everything. Ask him for help, but swear to all your Gods that you'll pay him back. Don't play on his feelings... Winter sighed. How was asking for his help *not* playing on his feelings? The last thing she wanted him to feel was that she was using him.

"I don't know what the hell to do." Saying it aloud helped.

Later, Winter kept up a performance as Raziel visited. He kissed her cheek. "Thank God they finally allowed me to visit you, darling. I don't mind telling you... I was getting a little annoyed. I don't like to be told no as you know."

There was a threat implicit in his words, and Winter studied the man she had somehow fallen into a relationship with and saw the monster within. *Play nice, keep him on your side.*

"Well, that's all over now. But they are keeping me in for further tests. I keep having chest pains, so they're just making sure."

Raziel took her hand in his and kissed the back of her fingers. "It's for the best, I suppose, but I can't wait to have you home. Listen, since everyone thinks we're engaged, why don't we make it official?"

Oh shit. "Raz, we barely know each other."

He smiled. "Come on now, Winter. I know everything there is to know about you. *Everything.*"

Did she imagine it or did his eyes drop to her belly? *Oh God, no...* she tried to smile. "There's not much to know."

"I know that I'm in love with you. I want you as my wife, Winter, and you know I always get what I want."

Winter fought the rising panic inside her as he pressed his lips to hers. "I don't want an answer tonight, Winter. You think about it. If nothing else, your financial future would be secured."

"I'm no golddigger."

Raziel laughed. "Who said you were? I'm offering you the world, Winter."

You're offering me a prison, she thought with a heavy heart. "You're too kind." She swallowed hard. "My sister..."

Raziel's face showed sympathy. "Both Autumn and your aunt were quick to tell me that they wanted nothing more to do with you. I'm so sorry, darling, but they don't deserve you."

A jolt of pure horror had gone through Winter, but not at the implication in his words. "You spoke to Helga?" Her voice shook as she stared at him. Raziel nodded.

You spoke to my dead *aunt? Liar...* Right then she knew she was in serious, serious trouble. What kind of psychopath was he? *Oh, dear God...*

He kissed her again, stroking her cheek with his finger. "I always get what I want, Winter," he repeated, and there was an edge to his voice that made her shiver.

RAZIEL STAYED for a couple of hours, and as the minutes ticked by, Winter felt the desperation build in her body. Finally, when he left for the night, she waited until she guessed he was well on his way home, then took out the cell phone.

Satchel answered on the first ring, and Winter felt like crying when she heard his soft voice. "Satchel... I'm sorry, I hate to ask but I need help. I really, really need help... please... I don't know what to do."

And she began crying. She heard Satchel's intake of breath, then as he spoke, a small ray of hope began to form in her chest.

"Sweetheart, don't cry, it's okay. I know exactly what to do."

END OF PART One

18
_____

CHAPTER EIGHTEEN

E leven months later...

WINTER SMILED AT HER PUPILS. "Okay, kids, that's it for today. Great work. I mean it, you're going to knock this Thanksgiving concert out of the park."

Her class, a group of preteens, laughed and clapped. "Instruments away now, lovelies."

She helped them tidy the music room, then said goodbye to each of them as they left the class. Winter glanced at the clock. Just after three-thirty p.m. Usually she would have loved to continue the class, but today was special.

Today, she would pick up her three-month-old daughter, Sukie, from the nanny and go straight to her friend's home for dinner. Cosima Forrester had been her lifeline in New Orleans ever since Satchel had spirited Winter away from Portland in the middle of the night eleven months ago.

Cosima—and her husband, Arlo—had taken Winter in, found her a job teaching at one of the city's music schools, and helped immeasurably as Winter's pregnancy progressed. With five children themselves ranging from three to thirteen years old, Cosima was a godsend as Winter struggled to come to terms with the fact that she was going to have a baby, a child fathered by a man she feared, who would almost certainly try to hunt her down.

Which was why Satchel wasn't with them here in New Orleans. Since the whole scandal had broken in Portland with Raziel under investigation by the FBI, Satchel had known he was under surveillance by Ganz's people and that he could so easily be traced to Winter. Raziel Ganz would come after her... and God forbid, come after his daughter.

If there was one thing Winter had been sure about from the start, it was that she didn't want her daughter anywhere near Raziel Ganz.

COSIMA GREETED them both with a smile, kissing Winter's cheek and Sukie's little head. "I swear she gets bigger every time I see her—which has been far too long, this time." She gave a mock glare to Winter who rolled her eyes.

"Dude, I saw you just last week."

"Still too long."

Arlo, Cosimo's gorgeous husband, came into the room. "Win, don't listen to her. She's all hormonal and broody." He tickled Sukie's cheek. "Which is entirely your fault, munchkin." But he said it with such a sweet fondness that Winter knew he was teasing.

"Dad says they have enough monsters already." Mina, the couple's eldest child grinned at her pseudo-aunt and Winter laughed.

"If all monsters were like you, Min-min, I'd have a bunch." Winter hugged her little 'niece.'

Cosima bore Sukie away from her mother and cuddled her. She batted her eyelashes at Arlo, who grinned. "Nope."

Cosima pretended to grumble. Winter's body relaxed. She loved being around this family. In the few months she had known them, she had been wrapped in their cocoon of love and laughter, and it was addictive.

Not that she didn't love her own little apartment. Just outside the French Quarter but away from the tourist traps, her apartment was small, compact, and had everything she could ever want. Satchel had insisted on it, but she made him swear she could pay him rent—he reluctantly agreed—but somehow, the rent seemed paltry in comparison to the apartment's specifications.

Winter remembered walking in, and it was as if Satchel had read her mind when it came to décor. Simple, cozy, the walls filled with bookshelves, the sofas large and comfortable. The nursery had everything a newborn could want, and when Winter had brought Suki home from the hospital, life had been simpler because of Satchel's thoughtfulness.

But she missed him. They talked nearly every day, still using the burner phone he'd given her in Portland. Lately, though, they'd been video chatting, sometimes late into the night.

THEN...

WINTER STILL REMEMBERED the night Satchel had come for her; he had everything organized for her to get away from Portland, away from Raziel Ganz. When Winter had asked Satchel for help, she had been totally honest. "Satchel... I'm pregnant with Raziel's baby. I don't want him to know or to have anything to do with the child. I have this feeling that... God, I'm going to sound crazy, but I have a feeling he's a dangerous man."

"Don't say another word," Satchel warned. "He may be listening somehow. Listen, I can get you away, but you have to be ready to do everything I say. From now on, just answer yes or no, understand?"

"Yes."

Satchel ran through everything with her, and she realized he must have been planning this safety net for her. Did Satchel know something about Raziel she didn't?

AT THE MOMENT OF ESCAPE, she had simply gathered her things—what she had left, which wasn't much—and headed for the hospital cafeteria. She was aware of Raziel's security guard following her, and although it irritated her, she didn't confront him. She remembered Satchel's words.

Get coffee, sit down. After ten minutes, go to the bathroom. We'll be waiting.

She did exactly as she told, keeping her movements relaxed and casual. To her relief, the security guard didn't even attempt to follow her into the bathroom, but when she got there, it was empty.

Winter found herself trembling; it was late, and the hospital gown and slippers were thin in the cool of the night. Then she saw a woman approach her. "Winter?"

She nodded, and the woman smiled. "Cosima Forrester. We're here to get you out of here."

Cosima wrapped a thick coat around her and pulled the hood up. She handed Winter a pair of jeans and some sneakers. "Put these on and we'll go. Your little buddy is being distracted as we speak."

As Cosima led her out of the bathrooms and away down a corridor, she heard raised voices behind her. "We paid an actor to act out someone with mental health issues. He picked a fight with Ganz's man."

Winter, bemused, smiled at the other woman. She was beautiful with dusky skin and big brown eyes... Indian-American, Winter guessed. She hustled Winter into the back of a car with tinted windows, and they were off.

They drove straight to the airport and to a private jet waiting on the tarmac. Inside, Winter gave a cry of happiness as Satchel stood to greet her. He was with another man who nodded at her, then he and Cosima gave Winter and Satchel some privacy.

Satchel held out his arms almost shyly, and Winter went into them. They held each other for what seemed an age, and for the first time in a long time, Winter felt safe.

"Thank you..." Her eyes were full of tears. "I had no right to ask you for help but thank you, thank you."

Satchel pressed his lips to her forehead. "Sweet Winter."

"You saved my life," she said simply, "I know it in my bones."

"Come sit down, and I'll run through what's happening next."

They sat, fingers entwined. "You'll fly to Canada and then down to the Caribbean just to make sure no one is following you. Then, Cosima and Arlo will take you to New Orleans. Everything is waiting for you there, darling. I'll call you tomorrow..."

"Wait... you're not coming with me?" The panic was back now, and she felt breathless.

Satchel closed his eyes and leaned his forehead against hers. "I can't," he whispered, "God, knows I want to, but I can't. It could mean him finding you. I'm more into this than you know..."

"Tell me." The thought of being away from him was killing her.

So, Satchel told her everything, about the FBI, about Raziel's alleged human trafficking. Winter was less shocked than she ought to have been. She nodded and told him about her theory that Raziel had been behind her houseboat being torched. "I think he did it, so he could look good 'saving' me. I think he paid someone to set off the fireworks, knowing they would freak me out, and then someone set fire to my boat." Winter sighed, the relief at being able to talk about it a palpable thing. Unconsciously, she placed a hand protectively over her belly as she spoke, and Satchel put his hand over hers.

"I won't let him hurt you or the baby, Winter, I swear."

Winter's tears fell then. "I'm so sorry to have to ask you, Satchel... I'm not using you, I swear. I just don't know where to go. If I go to my sister, he'll find me. And he'll hurt everyone I love." She met his gaze. "Please, Satchel... get out of this situation. Don't let him hurt you, too."

"If it brings him down for good, Winter, then it will all be worth it. You can be free. *We*... can be free."

She couldn't help herself then. She pressed her lips to his, kissing him hungrily, feeling his arms tighten around her as they embraced. That kiss, that sweet kiss... in it she found the answers to all the questions she had been asking, and she knew this man, this was her person...

CHAPTER NINETEEN

 ow...

WINTER BLINKED as Cosima grinned at her. "I'm sorry, Cos, I was daydreaming... what did you say?"

"I said I hope you've made up your mind about Thanksgiving? Mina's already made the guest room up for you and Sukie."

Winter smiled at the young girl. "Then how can I say no? But I do insist on helping with the cooking and decorating and everything I can."

Mina nodded enthusiastically. Since meeting Winter, the young girl had bonded with her, sharing her love of playing the piano and reading with Winter. Winter felt like she had a younger sister in Mina, and the teenager had such a sweet nature, and she reminded Winter of Summer so much, she almost mixed the two in her head.

She spent a wonderful evening with the Forresters, laughing at the antics of Mina's young twin siblings, Tilly and Fen, who mercilessly ragged each other and their father. Arlo, forever patient, rolled his eyes while Cosima joined in with the teasing.

Winter's heart hurt so much, both with joy and pain. She longed to see Autumn. Knowing that Raziel had lied about Autumn not wanting to see her when she had been in the fire... She knew the papers hadn't reported her name, and she wondered now if Autumn had ever even been told. *God, Auttie, I miss you so much.*

"Hey, you okay?" Cosima touched Winter's arm. "You're very distracted tonight."

"I know, I'm sorry. Being here with you all... it's just so peaceful, so loving, that it makes me think of what it was like, you know, before the... mall thing." She couldn't bring herself to use the word 'massacre'—it would sully this loving home.

Cosima, who knew all about being shot, nodded sympathetically. "I know. Listen, you know, if you ever need to talk about that, you know where I am. Anytime."

Winter smiled at her friend gratefully. "Thank you... but I don't want to bring up any bad memories for you, either."

"Pah, that was so long ago now, I can barely remember it." Cosima waved her hand, smiling, but then her smile faded. "Give yourself time. It does get better, I promise. The physical stuff? You know as well as I do that it heals quicker than the emotional stuff. It's only been a few years."

WHEN WINTER FINALLY WENT HOME, Sukie was fast asleep in her arms in the cab and didn't wake even as Winter laid her down in her crib. Winter sat by her daughter's side as she slept, wondering over the perfection of her features: her dark hair, her light olive skin, and bright blue almond-shaped eyes. Sukie Summer had been born a healthy weight and size, and although Winter had been scared she would not bond with her daughter because of who the father was, all doubts were erased at the moment Sukie had been lain on her chest.

It was a fierce, all-consuming love she felt for her daughter, and she had known in that moment that she had made the best decision she could have for herself and for her daughter.

To her surprise, Cosima had been with her throughout the birth and the days following. The Forresters had insisted Winter stay with them until she felt able to look after herself and the baby, and they were wonderfully supportive when she told them she wanted to start living an independent life.

And then there was Satchel. Every night he would call her, ask after Sukie, forever sending gifts for Winter and the baby. They would talk late into the night, about anything and everything. Winter told him about her sisters, her aunt... She told him about Summer, how much she missed her, and in turn, Satchel would tell her about his own family, his fun relationship with his stepmother and his love for his father.

He called as Winter was climbing into bed, and she smiled down the phone. "Let's video message, Satch. I want to see your face."

So, she grabbed her laptop and in moments, his smile lit up her heart. His green eyes sparkled at her, his handsome face now wore a thick, dark beard that had been growing for a few days now. God, his smile... it made her stomach warm, and she touched the screen. He grinned and put his hand up to the camera, too.

"Hey, beautiful."

"Hey yourself, big guy. I like the beard. You going undercover?"

Satchel laughed. "Something like that. How are you?"

Winter grinned at him. "In the last twenty-four hours? Same old, same old. Cosima invited me to spend Thanksgiving with them. God, it really has been a year already." She touched the screen again, making sure he could see the gesture. "And almost a year since I've seen you, my..." She'd nearly said it out loud, the way she thought of him, what she felt for him, but she didn't want to say it over the video messaging service. She smiled at him. "My sweet Satch."

He grinned. "Look, I have to tell you... the trial date has been set. Four weeks. Raziel will go on trial for trafficking, money laundering... but his lawyers are good. He's out on bail, and we have intelligence that he's looking for you still. His spies are everywhere; he has unlimited resources, and he's having me followed everywhere."

Winter's heart sank. He was telling her it would be a long time until they could be together in the kindest way he could. Besides... was that what he wanted? Or had she built up this scenario just from that one kiss, and from all the incredible acts of kindness and generosity.

She drew in a deep breath. *Risk it.* "I wish I could hold you, is all."

Satchel's eyes softened. "You don't know how much I wish I could make that happen, Winter."

Her body flooded with love. "Is this crazy, Satch? I know how I feel about you, but anyone looking in would say it's madness. We've only ever been in the same room three times."

He smiled. "Actually... no. We haven't."

Winter blinked. "What?"

Satchel looked away from the camera for a moment, then nodded. When his gaze returned to hers, his eyes were serious now. "I haven't told you this before, but now I think it's time." He attempted a smile. "And then you can decide if I'm the biggest creep in the world."

"Would never happen," she shot back with a laugh, but his face was still serious. "What is it, baby?"

"When... when you were in the hospital... after you had been shot. I visited everyone who had been injured. But you were the one whose injuries had been... They hadn't expected you to survive."

Winter nodded. "I know."

"After visiting hours... I'm ashamed to say I paid the nurse off to let me sit with you. Against your family's wishes. But I needed... I wanted to will you to get better, to get strong, to live." Winter saw him swallow hard. "I held your hand, your little hand. That's all I did; I held your hand. I would have swapped places with you in a heartbeat, Winter. I so desperately wanted to. I'm sorry if that seems... I know it could be misconstrued as..."

Tears were pouring down her face. "That was you?"

"I'm sorry," he said, misreading her meaning. "It was a terrible intrusion and—"

"No. No." She was shaking her head. "I *felt* you. I knew someone was there that whole time I was in a coma. Autumn and Helga thought I was crazy when I woke up and asked them where 'he' was. I told them, I knew it was a male presence in the room with me the whole time. God... Satchel..."

As she wept, she splayed her hand flat on the screen and Satchel put his hand up to hers. "Sweetheart, I didn't mean to make you cry."

"They're happy tears," she said, gulping, trying to catch her breath, "I swear they are. It just... you are..."

"I am *yours*," Satchel said simply. "Forever yours... if you want me."

Winter half-laughed, half-cried. "Forever?"

"Forever. We just have to make sure your forever is a safe one first."

Winter nodded. "I understand but know this. Sukie... if it wasn't for her, then I'd say screw it, because one more moment with you is worth dying for, Satchel Rose."

He winced. "Don't say that, baby." Then his face softened. "But thank you for saying it. I feel the same way... I want to say more but not over a wireless connection."

Winter laughed. "I agree." She traced the curve of his face with her finger. "But God, I wish I could touch you."

They talked for another couple of hours until finally they said goodnight. After she watched Satchel break the connection, she smiled. "I love you," she whispered into the ether and closed her eyes, giving in to sleep and to the most pleasant dreams she could have wished for.

CHAPTER TWENTY

R aziel Ganz sat in his newly acquired offices in Portland, listening to what his lawyer was saying. He wasn't worried about the spurious (his words) FBI investigation. Every possible witness had been paid off or had simply disappeared, and the case would be laughed out of court.

He'd known about the investigation, of course, even suspected that the FBI had a man on the inside. When Winter had disappeared from Portland General, he had known exactly who helped her do it.

Satchel Rose.

He had suspected some kind of relationship between them from the start. The first night they had met on his boat, he had watched them talking for a while and the connection between them, even in that brief moment in time, was obvious.

Raziel, of course, had arranged to have Winter followed everywhere, and when she met with Rose in that bookstore, he sat with his teeth grinding together as his spy described it to him. "They were holding hands, boss. Didn't look like a random meeting to me."

Bitch. Raziel had toyed with having them both killed, but instead he was patient. Winter would be his... but her sister being so well-known complicated matters. Autumn Mai might be estranged from her sister but if Winter disappeared—and Raziel knew she would make him a fortune if he sold her—Autumn Mai wouldn't rest until she found her.

Instead, he planned on making Winter stay with him, using subtle threats and isolating her from her few friends here in Portland —especially Satchel Rose. A part of him couldn't blame Rose for desiring what belonged to Raziel. Winter was beautiful, sweet, intelligent—any man would want her.

And of course, she was a spectacular fuck...

He'd made the mistake of underestimating her, though. When she had disappeared from the hospital, he had been incensed. But money was money, and he was using his to scour the world for her.

Wherever she had gone, she was well hidden. Raz knew Satchel Rose was the key to finding Winter, but just as he had begun to search for her, the FBI had closed in. He was certain Rose had something to do with that, too.

No matter. This nuisance of a court case would go away, and he would find Winter. He'd make her life hell until she understood that Raziel always got what he wanted. He might even make her think he would spare her life for a while, lull her into a false sense of security before he had the pleasure of killing her... slowly... and with his own hands.

Gareth knocked once and stuck his head in the door. "Got a moment, boss?"

"For you, always." Now more than ever he appreciated the loyalty of his staff. Gareth, Davide, the rest of them. Not one had bailed out when he was arrested and indicted. They'd all been subpoenaed which made Raziel laugh. The FBI were clutching at straws.

Gareth came in and sat down. "That journalist keeps calling."

"The girl? Mallory something?"

"Kline."

Raziel sighed. "She's been on my ass for months now, since before Winter disappeared. She knows I won't talk about it."

"Well, you may want to. Seems Autumn Mai is finally stepping up her own search for her sister and sooner or later she'll find out about you and her sister. Autumn Mai will come for you.'

Raziel shrugged. "So? She's a glorified muffin peddler. No one who can bother us."

Gareth said nothing and Raziel raised an eyebrow. "You think she's a threat? Be honest."

"Raz... we underestimated Winter, too. Autumn Mai might look like a soft threat but believe me, she's anything but. This is a woman who broke the glass ceiling in her field. She lost her sister in the St. Anne's Massacre, lost her aunt—who brought the girls up—just last year, and now Winter..."

"Wait, what? The aunt died?"

Gareth nodded. "Just before the fire."

"Fuck." Raziel remembered what he'd told Winter in the hospital. She would have known he lied...

"What is it?"

Raziel shook his head. "Nothing. So, what does Autumn Mai have to do with this journalist?"

"They're working together. Might not be the best time to shut down an interview. Press is always important. If Kline's an ambitious journalist—and which one isn't—then she could go full *anti*. Best get on her good side."

"Or we could just get rid of her."

Gareth gave his boss a chilly smile. He'd never had a problem telling truth to power. "The fewer bodies piled up around us right now, the better, don't you think?"

Raziel's mouth hitched up in a smile. "This is why I pay you, right?"

"Right. So... let's set a preliminary meeting with Kline. Get her to tell you what she wants, get a read on her motives."

"Fine. Let me know when and where."

"Also, you have to check in with the court this afternoon."

"I know. Thanks, Gareth."

. . .

RAZIEL WAITED until he was alone before he searched the internet for every fact he could glean about both Mallory Kline and Autumn Mai. A half hour later, he knew he had to be careful with both of them. They were forces to be reckoned with and if Autumn was trying to find her sister with the same tenacity he himself had searching for Winter...

This time, he knew he had to deal with things head on. Gareth was right. The fewer bodies around them, the better.

He'd make one exception to that rule. Satchel Rose would pay for taking Winter away from him.

He would pay with his life.

CHAPTER TWENTY-ONE

F all had settled in around New Orleans, and the weeks flew by until Thanksgiving came around. The afternoon before, Winter's pupils performed at a concert in their school auditorium. Winter had to be careful to stay out of sight of the local press who were taking pictures of the young performers, but she made sure they all knew how proud she was of them. They in turn showered 'Miss Woods' with boxes of chocolates and flowers, their grateful parents singing her praises.

That's who I am now, she thought to herself. *Winnie Woods.* It still felt alien and a part of her ached to be able to be herself again—to reclaim her name.

She shook the thought away. *It was worth it to be here, to be safe.* And now she had a few weeks of vacation to relax and spend time with Sukie. She picked her up from the sitter after school closed and went home. She bathed herself and Sukie and dressed them both up for the festivities at the Forrester's, briefly smiling at how she borrowed and amended that name for her own pseudonym.

She packed a case for the two of them, marveling at just how much she had to pack for her daughter.

"For a little bean," she said to the gurgling baby, wriggling on top of the coverlet of her bed, "you sure are high maintenance." She tickled Sukie's chubby little belly and nuzzled her own nose against her daughter's. "I love you so much, Sukie Summer."

Sukie grabbed a handful of Winter's hair and stuck it in her mouth and Winter laughed. "Minxy. Come on, let's get your coat on; the cab will be here soon."

She laughed as the cab pulled up to the Forrester's and grinned at Cosima who came out to help her. "Really? A Christmas tree already?" Outside the house, a huge spruce was covered in multicolored lights twinkling in the twilight. Cosima rolled her eyes.

"It'll teach Arlo and I to make bets with the kids that we won't win. I tell you, those darn twins..."

"They're nine and already they have the upper hand?" Winter mock-grimaced towards Sukie. "Just so you know, kiddo, Momma's always the boss."

"Ha, you say that now..." Cosima steered Winter into the house. "Harpa and Mikah are already here," she told her. Harpa was Cosima's younger sister, and Winter had met her a few times.

Harpa, as cute as her sister was beautiful, hugged Winter and cooed over Sukie, stealing her from Winter's arms. Winter hugged Mikah, Harpa's boyfriend. "So, no kidlings yourselves yet?"

"Ha. Not a chance," Harpa said, cuddling Sukie. "Why should we when we have six gorgeous ones here... well, four gorgeous ones and then the devil twins..."

She glared at Tilly and Fen who both grinned widely, their mouths already stuffed with food. Their six-year-old brother Bear waved at Winter. He had his three-year-old brother Henry on his back, carrying him around. Henry yelled his hellos loudly.

Cosima let Winter help her with the food as Harpa—a professional chef—sat on the counter and chatted to them. Cosimo occasionally looked pointedly at her sister as they got harassed by her on the preparations of the feast, but Harpa didn't take the hint. Finally, they sat down to dinner, and Winter once again felt the warmth of a family love. They had accepted her so readily, so lovingly, that it made her heart hurt. She wondered how Autumn was doing... could she risk a phone call?

She looked over at Sukie in her crib. *No.* There was no way she could compromise Sukie's safety for a quick phone call. Suddenly she felt lonely, even with her love for the Forresters.

"Hey, you okay?"

Winter smiled at Cosima. "I'm good. Just reminiscing."

"I'm sorry, lovely. I know what it's like to be estranged from family." She nodded at Harpa. "Harpa and I haven't seen or talked to our mother in years. She lost the right to be called our mother a long time ago. But that's different from you and Autumn. I truly believe that when Ganz is finally behind bars, you'll find your way back to each other."

Winter thanked her. Her words carried weight, and Winter allowed herself to think of a time when Sukie would know her famous aunt—and when Winter could hug her sister again.

...and when she and Satchel could be together. Even the thought of it made her body crave his touch.

"Hey, Winter?"

Harpa brought her back to the present. "Sorry, yes?"

Harpa hesitated. "I just wanted to say... I'm in New York for a conference next week and Autumn is speaking. I know getting a message to her is too risky, but I could... check in."

Winter nodded. "Yes, please. Just make sure she's okay."

"I will, honey."

"Don't mention Winter," Cosima warned her sister who rolled her eyes.

"Dude, I'm in my thirties."

Cosima grinned. "And still a brat."

Harpa grinned, sticking her tongue out at her older sister. "Always mothering me."

"Sorry," Cosima grinned sheepishly but Harpa shook her head.

"No worries, Cos. Makes up for..." Harpa smiled, and the sisters shared a moment of understanding between them. Winter smiled. This was family.

The night was full of fun and laughter, and the mood affected everyone. Even Sukie, cuddled and fussed over, seemed to pick up on it, giggling and gurgling happily. When Winter put her down in her cradle, she kissed her daughter's head tenderly. "Sukie Summer... I don't care who your daddy is, you're mine and I love you so much. We're going to have a good life, baby, even if we have to struggle to make ends meet. We'll have so much love that we won't feel when our bellies are hungry or our bodies are cold. You and me, baby boo."

"You'll never be hungry or cold, I promise you that, my darling one."

Winter froze. No, it couldn't be. Slowly she stood up and turned to see him in the shadows, leaning against the door jamb. She gave a little gasp, her hands flying to her mouth.

Satchel came into the light and his eyes were soft, tender. "Hello, Winter."

CHAPTER TWENTY-TWO

W inter's body reacted before her brain, and she flew into his arms. Their lips met as tears poured down her cheeks. The kiss went on and on, those long months of longing faded away as they clung to each other.

When finally they broke apart, breathless, Winter shook her head in disbelief. "What are you doing here? *How* are you here?"

"Subterfuge and a lot of strange, small airports. But I had to see you." He stroked her hair away from her face. "God, just to hold you in my arms is heaven."

"Satchel Rose... I'm so grateful to you. I missed you so much, and it's not out of gratitude or obligation. I just missed you."

Satchel leaned his forehead against hers. "I missed you, too, Winter. I think I tried to deny it, scared my feelings would distract me and that Ganz would get to you. I found the need to protect you was overwhelming. But I know what you mean... This was inevitable. We were meant to be together."

He kissed her again, making her head spin. The feel of his fingers drifting up and down her spine was making her crazy, and she pressed her body to his before remembering where they were.

She giggled as he groaned when she pulled away. "I'm sorry, but my daughter is sleeping, and I don't want to scar her for life by making love in front of her."

Satchel laughed, then went to the cradle. "She is gorgeous, Winter."

Winter slipped her hand into his. "I only have her because of you, and that's something I'll never be able to repay."

Satchel kissed her temple. "Sweetheart, you owe me *nothing*. Look, you might be wondering how we organized all this. Well, I have another surprise for you... well, a request, actually. There's no obligation, but... I have three days here. I would love to spend it with you and Sukie. If you're up for it, we could fly somewhere private and spend that time together. I've made all the arrangements, so it would be safe." He touched her face. "I'm not expecting anything, Winter, and this isn't something you have to say yes to. I just want to spend time with the pair of you."

Winter studied him. "You want both of us?"

"Yes," he said simply. "I want to get to know *both* of you."

Winter was moved beyond words. "I'd love to. God, yes... I'd love to, Satchel."

She saw his shoulders slump with relief, and he bent his head to kiss her softly. "You don't know how long I've waited for this moment."

She smiled. "Actually, I do."

They both laughed. Winter stroked his cheek, studying every inch of his handsome face. It was as if she knew it better than she knew herself, every freckle, every small scar. His big green eyes were soft on hers. "You are my person," she whispered. "I think I have known it since before I even knew of you. I feel like something inside me has been waiting for you all these years."

Satchel nodded. "I know this is crazy, and if we were sensible, we'd take things slow, but screw it. We both know how fucking fragile life is, how it can change in a moment. Let's not waste one more moment."

.   .   .

COSIMA HUGGED WINTER, and Winter kissed her friend's cheek. "Thank you for this," she whispered. "You don't know how much it means to me."

Cosima smiled. "I do, honey. This has been a long time coming. Enjoy these few days, darling. Don't let anything get in the way of you and Satchel. Forget everything else, forget Raziel Ganz. This is *your* time." She bent down to kiss Sukie's sleeping head. "You know, we could look after her for the few days."

Winter smiled. "Thank you, but I'm still breastfeeding, and Satchel wants to get to know us both."

Cosima looked over at Satchel who was talking with Arlo. "He's such a good man."

"I know."

SATCHEL SETTLED them in a car with tinted windows and drove them to a private airport where a small jet was waiting. It was different from the one she had flown to Louisiana in. Satchel grinned at her surprise. "I told you, it's all been a game of bait and switch. Not using the same transport twice. I even wore a blonde wig once."

Winter giggled. "Really?"

"No, just kidding." Satchel stuck his tongue in his cheek and she giggled.

They got onto the plane and settled in for the flight. "So where are we going?"

"Just a little place on a private island. It won't be a long flight, but we are going the long way around to it."

He sat down next to her, buckled himself in and took her hand. He nodded over to the crib where Sukie slept peacefully. "She's such a good baby."

"She is. Very chilled out. *Most* of the time." Winter leaned her head on his shoulder, felt him kiss her hair. Was it okay to feel this happy? Could she trust that for the next few days at least, the biggest worry she would have is whether she would have time to shave her legs before she and Satchel made love?

God, a thrill flooded through her body at the thought of being intimate with him. She looked up at him, met his gaze. He nuzzled his nose against hers then pressed his lips to hers. "Just us. Just our little family for the next few days."

Winter smiled and nodded. "Just us."

THE VILLA WAS on the beach of a very small privately owned island, but it was luxurious in the extreme. Winter, carrying Sukie, walked slowly through it, exploring the state-of-the-art kitchen, the large living area. The bedrooms were huge, and the master bedroom had an enormous bed swathed in mosquito netting. There was a small nursery just off of it and Winter settled Sukie in.

Satchel, having dealt with their luggage, came in to see them. Winter, sitting in the rocking chair, was nervous. "I have to feed her... are you one of those men who have a Madonna complex?"

Satchel laughed softly. "No, honey, go ahead. You feeding your child doesn't make me want you any less."

Winter grinned. "Good. Just checking."

"I don't want to intrude though, so how about I go fix us some food while Sukie's having her supper?"

She nodded, grateful that he sensed her shyness about breast-feeding in front of him. This was so strange... They had not even made love yet and here they were acting like a family. *Satchel* had called them a family.

Was this nuts? Winter searched her feelings but could not find any reason not to believe this could be their future. Sukie suckled at her mother's breast, and Winter smiled down at her. "I love you, Sukie Summer."

When Sukie was fed, and Winter had bathed her and put her in the cradle, she quickly shaved her legs in the bathroom, feeling almost like a giggly teenager. Her body tingled, her skin felt electric with anticipation. She wrapped herself in new underwear and a robe and went to find Satchel. She found him in the kitchen, chopping basil. He grinned up at her. "Just pasta, I'm afraid. I thought it was too late for anything heavier."

"Pasta is perfect." Winter realized that she had no idea what the time was and glancing at the clock, she boggled a little. "It's almost five a.m."

Satchel grinned. "We're on island time."

Winter chuckled. "This feels like a dream, Satch. This whole thing feels like a dream."

"Go with it. I am."

Winter couldn't help but giggle at the mischievous look on his face. "You got a deal."

THEY ATE TOGETHER, watching the sun creep slowly into the sky and then, trembling, they walked slowly to the bedroom together. Winter felt a wave of nerves come over her, and Satchel noticed. "You know? I could do with a shower first. Join me?"

She nodded in relief. Slowly they peeled each other's clothes off and all of Winter's fears fell away. God, his body... broad shouldered, hard pecs with a smattering of dark hair across them. Flat stomach rippling with muscles and slim hips. And his cock... God, he was *huge.* Winter's fingers moved as if they had their own will, stroking the hot length of it against her belly. Satchel's eyes were sleepy with desire as his big, warm hands stroked her skin.

"Christ, you're exquisite," he said, then smiled. "I didn't think it would be possible that you would exceed what I've been fantasizing about... but I was wrong."

Winter let out a shaky breath as his hand dipped between her legs and began to stroke. "Satchel..."

They showered together, their hands exploring every part of each other's bodies. His mouth was hungry against hers. "I want you so much, beautiful..."

Winter let go the last of her reservations. "Take me, Satchel... make love to me, please..."

Satchel gave a long groan and swept her out of the shower, still soaking wet and onto the bed, covering her body with his. He kissed her until they were both breathless, then smoothed damp hair away from her face. "You are so beautiful, inside and out," he said, his voice full of emotion.

"If I am, then it's you who have made me beautiful. You make me so happy, Satchel, so, so happy..."

He kissed her again, then moved down her body, his lips trailing down her throat to close upon her nipples, each in turn, teasing and sucking at them until they were rock hard. When his tongue dipped into her deep navel she shivered with pleasure, and then his mouth was on her sex, his tongue lashing around her clit, his fingers pressing her legs apart. Winter gasped and moaned as the tension built in her body, and Satchel brought her to a shuddering, explosive orgasm.

Her body was still flood with endorphins as he rolled a condom down over his straining, enormous cock, and as he entered her, Winter's eyes filled with tears. Yes... yes, this was what she wanted, this beautiful man inside her. Her legs wound around his waist, her fingernails dug into his buttocks as they moved together.

Satchel's eyes never left hers, the connection between them cementing firmly at that moment: the trust, the love—an unbreakable thing. As he moved inside her, his pace increased as their excitement grew, and then they were clawing at each other, feral, uninhibited in their lovemaking.

Winter came again hard, her back arching up, her belly against his, and she saw his face as he too reached orgasm, his beautiful eyes full of love for her. They both caught their breath, but Winter begged him to stay inside her for a little while longer. "I've never felt like this about anyone," she said fervently. "You are my world, Satchel Rose."

His lips were fierce on hers. "You and me, Winter. That's all I care about. You, me, and Sukie."

She touched his face. "And it doesn't bother you that she's Ganz's daughter?"

"She's *your* daughter, Win. Yours."

Winter smiled up at him. "When I think that I wasted all those years hating you."

"For good reason." His smile faded. "You know I would do anything to bring Summer back, don't you?"

"I do, lovely man. And in a way, you have. You helped me protect her namesake, her niece."

Satchel kissed her. "The thought of you and Sukie being anywhere near Ganz... God."

"We're well away thanks to you." Winter was quiet for a moment. "I left the name of the father blank on her birth certificate. The only way he can prove he is her father is with a DNA test, which he *could* legally force me to do, I think. So, Sukie's existence needs to be kept from him forever, or at least until she's eighteen."

"Will you tell her who her father is?"

Winter sighed. "I have eighteen years to figure that out. With any luck, he'll still be behind bars."

"If we can get him there in the first place." Satchel sighed, sitting up. He drew Winter close as she sat up as well. "The FBI's case is weak, and they know it. Every possible witness who could sink him has either been paid off or disappeared."

Winter felt a wave of fear pass through her. "And he knows you were working with the Feds?"

Satchel nodded. "More than likely."

"God... Satchel, he could come after you." She studied his face, and he looked away from her. Winter's heart failed.

"Oh no... he's already tried?"

"Not implicitly. But he came to see me soon after we moved you to New Orleans. Wanted to know if I'd 'heard' anything from you. I played dumb, of course, but he knew it was down to me that you were gone." Satchel smiled down at her. "I have a hard time keeping my feelings for you out of my voice, my expression." He sighed, shaking his head. "He knows you're my weakness."

"God."

Satchel kissed her forehead. "But I know that you are also *his* weakness. So, at the moment, we have the upper hand."

Winter was quiet, and Satchel's arms tightened around her. "Win, I mean it. We hold all the cards. And for these few days, we're not going to think about the future, okay? This is our time."

CHAPTER TWENTY-THREE

Sukie gurgled happily as she lay on the rug in the bedroom. Winter blew raspberries on her belly, making her daughter beam at her. Satchel grinned at them both. "You were born to be a mother, Win."

"Ha, you wouldn't say that if you'd seen me just after she was born. I had no idea what to do. Thank God for Cosima."

Satchel chuckled. "I wish I could have been there for you."

"God, no," she grimaced, "it was a car crash down there. You'd have never touched me again."

"Ha," Satchel threw his head back and laughed, "Win, when we give Sukie a brother or sister, I'm going to be right there, believe me."

Winter stopped tickling Sukie. "What?"

Satchel's smile faded. "I mean... if you want more kids... with me?"

Winter felt her heart fill with love and her eyes with happy tears. "A whole bunch, Satchel Rose." She picked Sukie up into her arms, then went into Satchel's. "Like you said, we are a family."

Satchel stroked a finger down Sukie's little cheek. "I could adopt her. Informally, if a formal process would mean admitting who her father was."

Winter touched his face. "You have already done more for Sukie than any other man would. You saved her life by helping us to escape Ganz."

Satchel smiled. "Well, why don't we take this little one and explore the island? I'm sure we'll enjoy the peace."

THEY HELD hands as they walked down the beach. Winter looked over at her daughter, swaddled protectively in a sling around Satchel's chest. The tiny little sun hat protected Sukie from the sun's heat, and the little girl stared wide-eyed out at her surroundings. Winter grinned, touching her daughter's tiny nose. "This place is heaven," she said, smiling up at Satchel. "Let me guess... it belongs to you?"

Satchel shook his head. "No, a friend of a friend of a friend. Someone I trust arranged it all. Someone who knows better than to tell anyone where I am. Trust me, Win, even Cos and Arlo don't know where we are."

A frisson excitement went through her. "No one knows where we are."

"Nope."

"That's kind of... sexy."

Satchel chuckled. "We think the same way, Ms. Mai. But... later." He nodded down at Sukie, who had her thumb stuck in her mouth. "Little ears. Like you said, we don't want to traumatize our girl."

Our girl. Winter squeezed his hand. "Luckily, she sleeps through the night, which is amazing considering how you made me moan last night."

"And I'm going to do it again tonight." He bent his head and kissed her quickly. "Over and over..."

Winter grinned. "You know, Sukie Su has afternoon naps..."

"Naughty girl."

Winter laughed. "I am what you made me."

Satchel lifted her hand and kissed it. "You're right. This place *is* heaven."

"Our little piece of it."

He smiled. "You know it."

THEY EXPLORED UNTIL LUNCHTIME, then took Sukie back to the villa. Winter went to the bedroom to feed her while Satchel made lunch. The island was so peaceful; Winter heard only the waves upon the beach outside as she sat in the rocking chair feeding her. She leaned her head back against the head rest. *How I wish we could stay here forever, just the three of us.* She knew if she said as much to Satchel, he would move heaven and earth to make it happen... but they had a responsibility They needed to make sure Raziel was made to pay for his crimes, not just for their and Sukie's safety, but for all the people Raziel had kidnapped and sold into sex slavery.

The thought of those poor kids—the girls, the lost teenagers. All of them without the safety net she had been given. No, they had to bring Raziel down. She looked down at her daughter, as Sukie stopped feeding, asleep already as her head fell away from Winter's breast and rested on her mother's arm. Winter couldn't even imagine her darling girl being taken, being so abused, sold to a sick pedophile. It made anger swell up inside her.

She laid Sukie down to sleep, then went to find Satchel. He was grilling steaks, daubing them with garlic butter. A lush salad and a bowl of freshly cut fruit sat waiting on the table. He smiled at her, then frowned. "Why so serious?"

Winter shook herself. "Sorry. I was just thinking about Raziel's hatefulness. How dare he trade in human beings? How dare he decided if they live or die? Asshole."

Satchel shut off the heat to the grill and flipped the steaks onto the plate to stand. Wiping his hands, he came to her. "We're trying to stop him, I swear we are. He's just gotten very, very good at hiding his tracks."

Winter thought for a while. "I could testify. I could testify that he was violent with me... just the once," she added hurriedly when she saw the anger in Satchel's eyes, "and believe me, I defended myself."

She unconsciously touched her throat, remembering that day on Raziel's boat, the day she knew who he really was.

"Sweetheart, as much as that is a serious charge against him, you can't prove anything. It would be just your word against his, and then your cover would be blown. You come to court, and he would have an army of people following you. No, it would do no good."

Winter gave a frustrated hiss. "I feel so useless not being able to help. All I have been is an inconvenience. For you, for Cos and Arlo..."

"Don't ever say that," Satchel said fiercely. "All of us, we would do it all over again to keep you and Sukie safe."

"But I hate feeling like the damsel in distress."

"You are no such thing. All of us need protection at some time in our lives—*all* of us. We need other people... people who love us when we are at our lowest. Do you know how grateful I am that you came to me? You trusted *me*, of all people?" Emotion made him sound angry, and he stopped and took a breath. "It is not your responsibility to bring Ganz down."

"But it is. For Sukie. For all those girls."

"We *will* bring him down and then, together, you and I, we can help his victims. When all of us are free from his threat. Because, Winter, Ganz will kill all of us before he gives in. You, me, Sukie. There is not one iota of mercy in him."

Winter felt the tears come then, and Satchel held her tightly. "I swear," he said, his lips against her hair, "we will get through this, and we will make this right, sweetheart. You and me. We'll help every one of his victims."

A NEW FEELING hung over the rest of their time together, and although it was not sadness, it was a recognition of their commitment to each other and to their future. They talked endlessly, making plans for when they could truly be together. Where they would live, what they would do, how they would bring Sukie up to be the happiest, most fulfilled child. The brothers and sisters they wanted to give her.

And in between talking, they made love, exploring every physical sensation they could, every inch of the other's body, letting their instincts guide them. Winter had never felt closer to another human —except for Sukie, but that was different. The mother-child bond was unbreakable for her, and now, as she and Satchel made love, she knew she had found her true soulmate.

ON THEIR LAST night on the island, Sukie was asleep, and they sat out on the beach, watching the sunset. "This is the cheesiest thing," Winter said with a laugh, "and I'm loving every minute of it."

Satchel grinned. "Me, too." He drew her closer and kissed her. "I hate that we have to go home tomorrow, but I can't risk Ganz's people growing suspicious. They know I'm due to meet with the FBI in two days. If I don't show up, his team will know—or guess—that I'm with you, and they'll blanket the country."

Winter felt sick. "God, you will take precautions, won't you? I can't bear to think of something happening to you."

"I'll be fine, don't worry about me." Satchel got up and pulled her to her feet. "Now, Miss Mai, I don't intend to waste one more second of our time together... I'm taking you to bed..."

CHAPTER TWENTY-FOUR

Winter turned over in her bed, restless. Her dreams were filled with ecstasy: the feel of Satchel's hands on her body, his sweet kisses, the way his long, thick cock thrust in exquisite rhythm inside her; the feel of her thighs being pressed apart by the weight of his strong legs, his fingers splayed across the curve of her belly as they made love; his tongue caressing hers, then sweeping down her body and lashing around her clit until she was helpless, begging for release.

Winter opened her eyes and shivered. Two days. Two days ago, they had returned to New Orleans, and she had to say goodbye to Satchel, not knowing when she would be in his arms again. Tearing herself away from him had been a torment, but they both knew it was for the best... for now.

Still, as she cranked up the heat in her apartment and went to check on her child, she felt bereft. Her body craved his touch, her mouth wanted to feel his lips, her mind wanted to laugh and joke with him and make plans for their future.

Winter pushed the thoughts away and reached for Sukie. Her daughter was a little antsy, kicking her legs up and fussy for her breakfast. Winter grinned at her. "Greedy girl. Come on then. Let's watch some dumb TV while you eat."

She settled into the couch as Sukie latched onto her breast. Winter grabbed the TV remote and flicked on the television. A small shock went through her when she saw her sister Autumn being interviewed on the *Today* show. Autumn was schilling for her new book, but Winter was shocked to see her sister looking so... Winter didn't know the word for how Autumn looked. Depressed? Disheveled? Autumn, out of all the Mai sisters, who could hide her feelings better than any of them, who always presented an utterly professional face to the world... She looked... hollow. Empty. Winter's heart ached for her sister.

She got her answer shortly after. The interviewer, a kind-faced woman, gently asked Autumn about her private life. "I know you've been through several personal tragedies lately, with the death of your sister and aunt, and then the recent disappearance of your other sister. Is your book reflective of the new life you find yourself living now?"

Autumn hesitated, looking discombobulated by the question. "My family... my family might be gone physically, but they are always with me."

"Your youngest sister, Winter... she disappeared after a house fire in Portland, I believe?"

Autumn nodded, and Winter was shocked to see her eyes fill with tears. "I know she's out there somewhere... I feel it. I know she's alive somewhere, and I hate to think she's scared, or she thinks I don't love her. I do. I *do* love you, Winter," she was addressing the camera now, and the host looked vaguely shocked. This obviously wasn't scripted. "I love you so much and I'm so sorry I didn't come for you when you needed me. Please... Winter..." Autumn broke down then and sobbed. The host patted her shoulder awkwardly and cut to a commercial.

Winter found tears pouring down her own face. God, what she would give to hug her sister now, to try to comfort Autumn. Without thinking, she grabbed her burner phone and called the last number she had for Autumn.

Her sister answered on the first ring. At that moment, as she lost grip on her mother's nipple, Sukie gave a scream of frustration.

It jolted sense back into Winter's mind and she ended the call quickly, dropping the phone on the floor. God, what had she done? The phone came alive. Autumn was calling her back.

Shit, shit, shit...

Winter got up, holding her squalling child and ignoring the ringing phone. She went into Sukie's bedroom and shut the door, mentally shutting the rest of the world out. *What a stupid fucking mistake...* she could have ruined everything that Satchel, Cosima, and Arlo has worked and risked for her.

She cuddled her daughter to her chest, settling her back into her rhythm of feeding. Winter could feel her own heart beating fast, and she took a couple of deep breaths to calm down. She would have to get rid of the phone and tell Satchel what she'd done. Winter closed her eyes and prayed she hadn't just put her daughter in terrible danger.

RAZIEL ONLY HALF-LISTENED to everything his lawyer was telling him. He was thinking about the interview he'd seen that morning on the *Today* show. Winter's sister begging her sister to come out of hiding. He knew it was a false hope but still, on the off-chance Winter had seen the interview, too...

He'd had Autumn Mai watched for months, ever since Winter disappeared. The woman was protected, yes; she had her own staff of security, and the studio where she filmed her cookery show was like a fortress. But still, he'd had her home and office bugged, her phone tapped. But there had been nothing.

Maybe Winter was already dead. Maybe she'd thought suicide was the only way out, that death was her only escape from Raziel.

You're right about that, my beautiful Winter. He got up and stared out of the window of his office. *Wherever you are, I will find you, and you will be convinced that your place is with me for the small amount of time I'll allow you to live.*

And not with Satchel Rose... Goddamn that man. Gareth had persuaded him to hold off on Rose's murder. "It's too obvious just now," Gareth told him. "They would know it's you in an instant. At the moment, we have the upper hand. They haven't got any witnesses so they're grasping at straws."

"Mr. Ganz?"

Raz turned from the window, finally focusing on his lawyer. An obsequious little man, Trent Urban smiled at him. "So, like I say, they've not presented any more evidence. I have a good feeling about this. We may even avoid a jury trial if we..."

"If you're about to say we enter a plea, that's not going to happen, Mr Urban." Raziel's voice was old. "This investigation has been a farce from the start. The FBI needed some good publicity, and they decided to ruin my reputation to get it."

Raziel hadn't been stupid enough to cue Urban in on his actual occupation. The less his lawyer knew, the better. He had enough staff who knew the truth, and they were unfailingly loyal to him.

AFTER HIS LAWYER HAD LEFT, Raziel made some phone calls, but his mind was still on the interview that morning. Just after lunch, Gareth knocked on the door. He was smiling.

"What is it, Gareth?"

"What you always wanted, boss. Winter. *Possibly.*"

Raziel looked up. "What?"

"The sister's cellphone pinged with something. It may be nothing, but the call was dropped as soon as the sister answered. Then Autumn Mai tried to call the number back but there was no answer. We didn't have it for long enough to trace it, but here's the thing."

Raziel shifted impatiently in his chair. "Get to it, Gareth."

Gareth smiled. "The call came immediately after Autumn's little breakdown on TV. Wouldn't you think a long-lost sister who happened to see that heartbreaking performance would call her sister?"

Raziel nodded slowly. "Okay, but how does that tell us where Winter is?"

"It doesn't. And yes, we're working on suppositions, but it seems plausible. Which means Winter is somewhere in the United States still. And that just seeing Autumn cry almost made her break her radio silence."

Raziel stared at his secretary as understanding crept into his mind. "You said no murders, Gareth."

"Who said anything about murder? Just the appearance of peril and I guarantee, Winter will come skittering out of the shadows and then—"

"—she's mine."

Gareth nodded. "Yes."

Raziel tapped his pen on the desk for a moment. "What do you suggest?"

"You have a meeting in New York next week with Severs and Co. We call the journalist, Kline. She's been hankering for a sit down with you. Tell her if she wants it, she has to come to New York to do it; it's the only time you have. We have someone contact Autumn Mai, set a meeting with her for lunch somewhere we choose. They don't turn up. She's annoyed, frustrated, she runs out of the restaurant. A car, the driver up on the sidewalk, barely misses her."

Gareth leaned forward. "It barely misses Autumn. Just so happens you're passing. You leap out of the car. Kline sees you acting all heroic for the damsel in distress. Writes about it. Winter sees it. Gets the message. Her or her sister."

Raziel contemplated this for a long moment. "I didn't hide my relationship with Winter. What if Kline knows, sees through this?"

"You might not have hidden it, but it wasn't exactly public knowledge."

"Rose knew. Rose could make it public. So could the hospital."

Gareth shrugged. "So? It happens to be a coincidence. You could even play dumb with the sister."

"She's a well-known face."

"Since when do you have time to watch cookery shows? I know you told Winter you'd talked to Autumn and the aunt, but we both know that call was never made."

"Yeah, and that was a mistake. Winter knew I lied... would she have left if I'd been honest?"

Gareth gave a snort of frustration. "What does that matter now?"

Raziel sighed. "Okay, it's worth a shot. Set it up."

"Hey, baby."

Winter smiled at the laptop's screen and touched the image. Satchel grinned. "Hey yourself, beautiful."

They chatted easily for a few moments, then Winter took a deep breath and told him what happened. She tried to read his expression. "I'm sorry, Satchel. I lost control for a second. Do you think I've blown it?"

"You only left the connection open for a moment?"

"I would say less than ten seconds. Much less. Just enough time for her to say hello then I hung up. Do people still say hung up?"

Satchel half-smiled. "I do, but then I'm old."

"Hogwash."

"People definitely don't say *that* anymore." But he laughed, and Winter was relieved he didn't seem too concerned about her mistake. "Sweetie, I think we're okay just... maybe don't use that phone again."

"I won't. I went out and got another burner this afternoon. I'll text the number to you."

Satchel smiled. "I miss you."

"Oh, I miss you, too, Satch, so much." She grinned at him. "Especially at night."

He laughed. "Baby, I swear, this court case had better be over soon, or I'm going to go crazy." His smile faded. "Seriously, the important thing is you and Sukie are safe until Ganz is put away. Then we have the rest of our lives to spend together."

· · ·

AUTUMN MAI APOLOGIZED to the floor manager and the hosts of the show profusely and left the studio feeling embarrassed and humiliated. What the hell? She'd lost control, and she never did that, ever. But these last few months, hell, these last few years, ever since that day at the St. Anne's Mall. She could remember Helga taking that terrible call just as Autumn saw the initial reports on the television.

She remembered thinking 'There's no way... there's no way Summer and Win could be involved..."

But the red-and-blue flashing lights which showed up at her apartment, the officers with the studied, controlled sympathy... *God.* And now, despite her success, her wealth, her fame... she felt she had nothing. At work she put on her best face: professional, upbeat, inspirational. But every night she would go home, watch the TV unseeing, then crawl to bed and cry herself to sleep.

She knew her depression was beginning to show. It was spiraling, *had* been spiraling out of control since the news of the fire on Winter's houseboat. At first, even with her contacts, she'd been unable to find out which hospital Winter had been taken to, and by the time she'd tracked her sister down, Winter had disappeared.

Even her contacts around Portland turned up nothing. The people at the dockyard were curiously silent, with only the harbor master telling her that Winter seemed upset in the days before the fire. When she asked him why, she saw his expression shut down.

No. Someone was paying to keep secrets. Goddamn it. Autumn kept thinking back to that last phone call, when she'd told Winter about Helga's death, when her grief, guilt, and anger had taken over. Winter thought she, Autumn, had turned away from her... *what if, oh God help me, what if she thought she had no one and decided life wasn't worth living? What if she'd set the fire herself, tried to kill herself that way?*

Autumn gave an involuntary whimper as she sat in the green room of the studio, waiting for her car to arrive. She rubbed her face just as her cell phone buzzed and unthinkingly, she answered it without checking the number. "Hello?"

All she heard was a gasp and the sharp, quick wail of a baby before the phone went dead. Autumn barely had time to register the sound before the call was cut off. She glanced at the screen but didn't know the number. She called it straight back. No answer, and it went to voicemail, an automated voice telling her to leave a message. Autumn hung up without speaking. A wrong number? Probably.

But the whole time in the car home, something niggled at her about that call. The gasp, the baby's cry. Her mind worked overtime, and she argued it over in her head. Could it have been Winter? And if so... she had a child? It didn't seem like her sister to be a mother, but if she were, she certainly wasn't living the white picket fence American dream.

Where are you? She wondered if she could afford to spread her search wider. She was wealthy, yes, but she didn't have unlimited funds...

She needed to go back to Portland, start from there. Someone at that hospital must know something even if they had been paid off. At home she called her agent and asked him to postpone her work in New York for a couple of weeks. "It's important, Will. Family stuff."

Will, her literary agent, sighed. "Look, the best I can do at this late stage is cancel everything after Friday. But, Autumn, people have spent money, have changed their plans for the benefit tomorrow. Please tell me you'll be there, at least."

"Fine." Autumn was just grateful Will wasn't giving her too much of a hard time. "Listen, thank you, I know it's an imposition... but it's my sister, you know?"

Will's tone was softer when he spoke again. "I know, sweetie, I saw the show. Listen, anything I can do, just ask. Really."

Autumn gave a half-laugh. "Well, unless you have a private detective on staff..."

Will chuckled. "No, but I know a guy. I could call him."

"You know a guy?" Autumn smiled, her tone teasing. "Like on the down low? William Skye, you have contacts?"

He was laughing. "Don't bust my balls, Auttie, I'm just saying I grew up in Brooklyn. I know people."

"Well, I'd be grateful. You know money isn't a problem." She hoped that was true but at this point she'd mortgage everything she owned to find Winter.

"Give me a couple of days."

"Thanks. You're a babe."

Will laughed again. "Oh, I know, that's why you pay me ten percent."

AUTUMN BOOKED her flights for Portland, then went to decide what to wear for the benefit the following evening. Now in her midthirties, Autumn was mature enough to know she couldn't just blow off such an event, even if it was to go find her sister. She spent a half hour pulling out dresses from her walk-in closet but the whole time, she was thinking of doing this with her sisters... planning what to wear. Summer had been the most girly-girl of them all, Winter always the tomboy. Autumn liked beautiful clothes, but her focus was mainly her business rather than looking pretty.

Summer... Summer had always liked to look pretty, loving a retro fifties-style of dress, the type of clothes she had sold in her boutique in Seattle. Autumn remembered just how beautiful Summer had looked, even in death, lying so serenely in her casket, the bullet hole in her throat disguised by a scarf.

The funeral had been hell, not the least because Winter had been in a coma and not expected to survive. Everyone at Summer's wake had fully anticipated gathering together again very soon, but Winter had surprised them all.

Except... it hadn't been Winter who emerged from that coma. It was someone Autumn and Helga hadn't recognized. Gone was the zest for life, the girl who lived for her music and her family, who had so many hopes and dreams. Instead, a loner, an angry, bitter, resentful loner had appeared. A scared little girl. The thought that Winter might be scared now made Autumn's heart ache.

Autumn sank to the floor, her head in her hands. *I should have cared for you better, Win. I should have tried...*

Autumn fought off the tears and grabbed her phone. She flicked to her call log and redialed the last call number. After the auto-lady had done her thing, Autumn took a deep breath in. "It's me. If you're who I think you are, and if you're in hiding... just know I love you. I want to help you, whatever you need... you and whoever is with you." She stopped—her voice was shaking so much. "I mean it. I'm here for you. Whatever you need. All you have to do is get me a message. I don't know if you're in trouble, but I'm guessing you are. I'll never stop looking for you. I love you. Bye."

She ended the call... and burst into tears.

CHAPTER TWENTY-FIVE

"You're quiet, baby. Are you okay?"

Winter nodded. "Autumn left me a voicemail message. She guessed it was me, or rather she took a risk that it was me. She didn't say my name. God, Satchel, just hearing her voice wrecked me." She wiped at her face, the tears coming again. "Jesus, I'm always crying, what the hell is wrong with me?"

"Nothing, darling. This whole situation is fucked up." Satchel looked exhausted, and now Winter touched the screen, tracing the shape of his face.

"What is it?"

Satchel sighed. "The FBI thought they had a break in the case. They found someone who escaped from Raziel's henchmen. They found the body this afternoon."

"Oh God. Look, what do they have?"

"Nothing." Satchel's voice rose now. "They jumped the shark and went too soon, and Ganz saw them coming. This whole thing is ridiculous." He was angry, and Winter wished she could hold him, tell him everything would be okay... but that would be a lie.

"Satch..."

"—Ganz's lawyer is moving to have the case dismissed, and it looks like it will be." Satchel interrupted her, and his words came out in a rush. It was obvious that he had been trying to tell her all evening, and now it was out in the open.

Winter's whole body went cold. "No. No, they can't give up now."

"They have *nothing*. They kicked the wasp's nest without calling the exterminator. Ganz will never see the inside of a courtroom. *Fuck.*"

She had never seen him so angry, so despondent. She let him rant for a while until finally, he gave her a rueful grin. "Sorry to dump, baby."

"That's what couples do," she said softly. "And fuck this. Fuck Ganz. I want to be with you. Sukie needs her family together. You, me, Sukie and Auttie. If they're not going to put that man away, then I'm done hiding."

"No. No, we can't think like that. He'll still come after you."

"Let him."

Satchel touched the screen. "If anything happened to you, Winter..."

"What can he do that he hasn't already tried? He set that fire. I have no doubt that if I had stayed with him, I would have ended up an indentured sex slave for him. Or sold to the highest bidder, whatever." Suddenly a thought struck her. "Hey, your contact at the FBI..."

"Holbrook?"

"Yeah, him. Can I talk to him?"

Satchel frowned. "About what?"

"Well, maybe I can help. I hate just being the passive little damsel in distress. I'm tired of hiding. I want to be with you, I want to see my sister..." Her voice broke then, and she stopped, breathing deeply, trying to control her emotions.

Satchel waited until she had gathered herself. "Sweetheart... Ganz is far more dangerous than I think you realize. If you're suggesting what I think you are—using yourself as bait—it would achieve nothing but you putting yourself back into his crosshairs. No, I'm sorry, I'm not trying to be a controlling jerk about it, but it's too risky."

Winter sighed. "So, my life will be always looking over my shoulder? Never being with you?"

Satchel looked as distressed as she did, and he rubbed his eyes. "Look, it's the holidays soon... I'll try to figure something out, so we can spend them together. I want to be with you too, darling, so, so much. I'm just terrified he'll get to you."

Winter gave a sob. "How the hell did my life come to this?"

Satchel just shook his head and placed his hand against the screen. She put her hand to his. "I need you, Satchel."

"I'm here. Always for you, always."

RAZIEL GANZ SMILED WIDELY as his lawyers related the news that the case against him had been dismissed. "Good. Now I can get back to running my business."

He hung up the phone, and he and Gareth shared a smile. "So, what's next?" His assistant was shuffling pieces of paper, eager to get back to everyday work, but Raziel shook his head.

"Finding Winter is priority one."

Gareth sighed. "Really? Raz, have you thought about letting it go? I have this feeling that if you pursue this woman, it could all go down in flames. If, like you suspect, she's being hidden by Satchel Rose, then she's uber-protected. He won't let you near her."

"*Let* me? Since when has anyone denied me anything?"

Gareth stared at his boss, his eyes strangely nervous. "Raz, as your assistant, your friend, I'm telling you... this has become like an obsession for you. You really want to risk everything for one woman? What's so special about Winter Mai?"

Raz smiled coolly. "No one leaves me, Gareth. No one."

"And what if she won't come back to you?"

Raziel just stared at his assistant without speaking and saw Gareth give an involuntary shiver. Gareth knew exactly what Raz would do to Winter if she denied him. Raz smiled to himself. It was good to know his most trusted advisor could still be shocked by him. "Gareth, have you set up the meeting with Mallory Kline?"

"I have. She'll be waiting for you in New York and will accompany you to the benefit."

"Good." They had learned that Autumn Mai had cancelled all promotional duties due to 'personal reasons' and that she intended to come to Portland. Raz had changed the plan Gareth had come up with and instead was planning a charm offensive on his missing lover's sister. He wanted Mallory Kline to report that he and Autumn seemed 'close.' He knew Winter would understand his message.

He was just hoping Autumn would play along. His investigators had painted a picture of a woman who didn't suffer fools gladly. Raziel wasn't worried. He would have all the appearance of honesty when he met Autumn, concerned for Winter, but ready to move on— as soon as she knew what had happened to her.

What he wanted from Autumn was her trust, and the absolute one thing he knew he would do was turn her against Satchel Rose. That would give Winter a choice—her sister or her lover.

At least, that was what she would think her choice was. Raziel smiled to himself. What her actual choice would be was whether to live or die—and Raziel knew he would make her suffer either way.

Winter would be his whether she liked it or not.

CHAPTER TWENTY-SIX

Winter came home from work on Wednesday night and picked up Sukie from her sitter. Sukie was fussy, her color up, and Winter frowned, feeling her daughter's forehead and finding it hot. "Not getting sick, my love?"

The rest of the evening she cradled her daughter in her arms, dabbing at her forehead with a cool cloth and Sukie seemed to settle down. Finally laying her down to sleep in her crib, Winter realized her body was tensed up and tried to relax. The truth was, she still felt like an amateur when it came to motherhood, and despite Cosima's help, sometimes Winter wondered if she had done the right thing by keeping Sukie. Was it fair to her daughter?

She tried to push those thoughts away as she walked slowly around the apartment, tidying, keeping one ear on Suki's baby monitor, trying to shake the feeling that her life was spiraling out of control. Did she have any agency left now? She was living in an apartment paid for by a man, being told what to do by a man, her life one of secrecy *because of a man*...

"Fuck. Fuck, fuck, fuck." She wanted to scream and throw things. To distract herself, she flicked on the television and nearly fainted with horror. An entertainment show was reporting on a charity benefit in Manhattan the previous evening—and there, front and center, in the flash of paparazzi cameras, was her sister, Autumn—laughing and joking with *Raziel Ganz.*

"No. *No, no, no, no...*" Winter fell to her knees. She knew what was happening immediately—it was a threat. *Come back to me or Autumn is at risk. Jesus.* Winter felt numb, but a wail crept from her throat, involuntary, scared, terrified.

In her room, Sukie began to cry, and Winter, barely able to walk, crawled across the floor towards her daughter's room.

Suddenly she screamed as there was a frantic pounding on her door. She felt confused, her head foggy as Sukie screamed, and the panic in Winter's chest rose. She made it to Sukie's crib and grabbed her daughter, stumbling back to the door.

When she peered through the peephole and saw Satchel, a sense of calm descended. "What are you doing here?"

Satchel took a crying Sukie from her and steered Winter into a chair. Behind him, Cosima and Arlo followed, closing the door quickly behind them. Winter blinked, trying to understand what was happening. She clung to Satchel's hand, her focus on her distressed daughter. Cosima took Sukie from Satchel and began to calm her down.

Arlo went to the kitchen. "I'll make her some tea."

Satchel took Winter in his arms. She gazed up at him. "What are you doing here?"

"My people in New York told me about Ganz and your sister. I knew that when you saw it, you'd freak out." He gave her a half-smile. "And I wanted to see you."

Winter nodded, still discombobulated. She wanted to feel elation but all she could think of was her sister in Raziel's clutches. She held her hands out for her daughter, and Cosima gave Sukie to her. She saw Cosima and Satchel share a concerned look. "I'm okay," she mumbled, but she knew it was a lie. She couldn't feel anything but terror.

And weirdly, seeing Satchel was making it worse. Even though she craved him, wanted to be with him so badly, she knew he wouldn't have risked exposure unless the situation was already dire. He knew what it meant that Autumn was on Raziel's radar.

Somehow, between them, Satchel, Arlo, and Cosima managed to calm her down to the point where she could think. "He's targeting my sister to get me to come to him."

"Yes." Satchel nodded, his green eyes serious. "We can't give in to him."

"Enough people have died because of me."

Satchel frowned. "*No one* has died because of you. What the hell?"

"Summer."

Cosima shot Satchel a worried glance then crouched down and took Winter's hands. "She didn't die because of you, Winter. It was a cruel, random act of violence."

Winter stared at Cosima. "He'll kill her, Cosima. He'll kill Autumn if I don't give myself up to him."

"We're not going to let that happen." Satchel's arms tightened around her and Winter finally let her body relax.

"Look, we're going to take Sukie home with us for the night, give you two some time to talk. Is that okay?"

Winter nodded, kissing her daughter's head. Sukie had calmed down now, and as Winter pressed her lips to her little forehead, she noticed her daughter's head was cool and dry. One less thing to worry about.

COSIMA WAITED for Winter to express some of her breast milk to feed Sukie overnight and then the Forresters left. Winter felt a pull as she watched them take her daughter but knew she would be well looked after.

As the door closed, she looked at Satchel. "What the hell am I going to do?"

"*We.* What are *we* going to do, Win. We're in this together." He kissed her finally, quick, soft. Winter leaned into his body warmth.

"He's never going to stop, is he?"

Satchel shook his head. "No. He's relentless. He's ruthless."

They sat together in silence for a while before Satchel cleared his throat. "Winter... we could make us... legal."

"What?"

"If we were to be married, if Sukie was officially 'mine,' we could go public. Despite the charges being dropped, Ganz's investors are running scared. If he thought his reputation would suffer, he could be persuaded to leave you alone. It would mean going public, but it would also mean that we would have the protection of being in the public eye. Ganz wouldn't risk taking you if it meant he would be exposed."

"But how on earth would I explain Sukie?"

"We were 'having an affair while you were with Ganz.' That's how. You left him when you realized you were pregnant with my child."

"He could force a DNA test."

"He could, but again, he'll be concerned about the court of public opinion."

Winter shook her head. "I'm not convinced, baby. Raziel Ganz is ruthless and relentless. You said so yourself." She sighed and put her head in her hands. "But Autumn is in trouble, and I can't let her be fooled by him, be used by him. God, Satchel, what the hell are we going to do?"

"Right now? Nothing. I have people in New York looking out after Autumn. For now, for the holidays, we wait." He stroked her hair back behind her ear. "I swear to you, Winter, all of this will work out, even if we have to break some laws. I want to give you the life you deserve." He gave her a crooked smile. "And I do want to marry you."

Winter smiled for the first time. "And I you, but not like this. Not for this reason. I want to marry you in happiness, not in fear." Her smile faded. "Honestly, tell me the truth. Can you see this ending any other way than me going to Raziel?"

"I don't want that to happen."

"Neither do I... but," and she took a deep breath. "If it does... I'm prepared to do anything to make sure my daughter grows up happy, secure, and free." She met Satchel's gaze. "Anything."

CHAPTER TWENTY-SEVEN

Winter had fallen asleep finally, and Satchel lifted her up and carried her to the bedroom. She stirred as he laid her down on the bed. "Stay with me," she whispered pulling his lips down to hers. "Make love to me, Satchel..."

They undressed each other slowly, taking their time, kissing, caressing each other's skin. Satchel gazed down at her as he entered her and began to move. "You are my everything now, Winter."

"And you, mine," she said simply. She tightened her thighs around his waist as he began to thrust, her body filling with desperately needed endorphins as they made love. Despite this, she couldn't reach her peak, too disturbed by events and afterwards, they lay in each other's arms, quietly talking.

Satchel pressed his lips to her forehead. "I feel as if I'm to blame for how messy this is. Maybe I should have tried harder with the FBI to get you proper protection."

"That would have led to me not being able to make any of my own decisions, Satchel. You did everything you could—never say otherwise. In reality, I should have fought my own battles, gone to the police, made it clear to Raziel that I didn't want anything."

"But you were left with nothing after the fire."

She nodded. "And I believed Raziel when he said Autumn didn't want to know me. I really was penniless, homeless..." She smiled at him. "And you, my white knight, you saved me. But I should have taken the time to think things through."

Satchel was stroking her body. "What if you told your story to a journalist? Get that knowledge out there? It would restrict Ganz's ability to spin things the way he wants. And, with Sukie, I have an idea. I have a friend who is a family matters lawyer... we can go to her for advice."

"You haven't yet?"

"It's not my decision, Winter. Sukie is yours and I wouldn't presume. Which sounds ridiculous after all of this."

Winter chuckled softly. "Neither of us know what we're doing, do we?"

Satchel grinned. "Nope. So let's just take it back to basics. We want to be together, be a family. That is the basis of everything."

"Just add in an obsessed madman and hey ho, a fairy tale ending!" She joked but her laugh was shaky. "Satchel, if he harms Autumn..."

"He won't. He *won't*, Winter. From what I've seen of Autumn, she's no fool."

Winter chewed her bottom lip. "I need to talk to her. Tell him what Raziel is like. Sooner rather than later." She looked at Satchel. "I mean it. The more Autumn knows, the more she can protect herself, and I don't trust that she'll listen to anyone but me. Can you set something up?"

Satchel nodded slowly. "I can. But I want to wait a week or so."

"Why?"

"I want to see how Ganz is going to play this."

"No. Not acceptable, if he..."

"Nothing is going to happen in a week," he said firmly. "It's the holidays. Autumn is flying to Portland, and my people will be with her all the way. One of them is known to her, a journalist. She's the one who broke the news of their meeting at the benefit. She's working for me."

"Who?"

"Mallory Kline."

Winter shook her head. "I don't know her."

"She's a friend." He grinned suddenly at the jealousy on Winter's face. "*Just* a friend, I swear. She wants the big story, the story on Ganz's human trafficking, but while she's tailing him, she's staying close to Autumn and telling me what her movements are."

"God." Winter felt sick. "The surveillance."

"Non-invasive and at the moment, vital," Satchel said firmly. His expression softened. "Hopefully, soon, this will all be over. I don't want you, either of you, to have to live your lives under scrutiny."

He stroked her face and kissed her softly. "And it occurs to me in all of this, there's something I've never said to you, Winter Mai."

"What's that?"

He smiled. "I love you. I'm in love with you, so in love with you. When I met you, even if I didn't know it at the time, I found my true north, my partner—"

"—in crime?" Winter joked but her eyes were full of tears. "I love you, too, Satchel. I knew it the night on the boat, even when I threw that drink on you." She gave a half-laugh, half-sob. "So many emotions. It seemed cruel that the man I hated for so long—for no reason—would suddenly turn out to the person I had been searching for. Over these last few months, God, I have been in turmoil, every night I couldn't wait to talk to you, to see you. You're my best friend, Satchel Rose, and I want to spend the rest of my life showing you how much I love you."

There was no need for words then as Satchel's mouth found hers, and they began to make love again, intense and focused—no inhibitions.

This time, Winter had absolutely no problem coming hard and long. She clung to Satchel as if she never wanted to let him go—which was the truth.

NEITHER OF THEM slept that night, making love and talking, planning, trying to figure out a way to secure their future. Eventually, exhausted, Winter put her hand on Satchel's chest. "I have to go back to Portland. Let's face down Raziel and end this. I'm not hiding anymore."

Satchel looked unhappy but nodded. "I hate to say it, but yes, I think this is the only way." He was silent for a while. "Listen... I have a suggestion, and I know I've said this before but... marry me. Let's go back as a family. I know people. I know we can get Sukie a fake birth certificate..."

"Then why not a fake marriage certificate?" Winter stroked his face. "I meant it when I said I don't want our marriage to be one of necessity or as a reaction to Raziel. When I marry you, Satchel Rose, and I will say yes when the time is right, I want it to be an occasion of joy, with nothing sullying it."

Satchel nodded, frowning at first, then relaxing as she explained her refusal. "I get it. And I agree. I don't want Sukie and our future kids to ever ask about our love story and hear we got married because it was convenient or a way to stay alive."

Winter's eyes were full of tears. "Our *future* kids..."

"You know I love Sukie like she was my own."

"You are a remarkable man, Satchel Rose. To embrace your enemy's child—"

"She's not Ganz's child. She's the daughter of the love of my life, Winter. I've known it since before I realized it."

Winter kissed him then, and they began to make love again, strengthening their bond, celebrating the love between them.

LATER, when she was sure Satchel was asleep, Winter slid from the bed, snagging Satchel's phone from the nightstand and padding quietly into the living room, shutting the door behind her. She flipped through his contacts until she found the number she was looking for, then dialed it, keeping her other ear tuned to any noise from the bedroom.

When the call was answered, she felt a thrill of adrenaline go through her. "Agent Holbrook? You don't know me, but my name is Winter Mai. I need your help."

CHAPTER TWENTY-EIGHT

W inter could feel Mallory Kline sizing her up as the two shook hands. They sat down in the small hotel room in Portland, and Winter offered the other woman a drink. "No, thank you. Maybe later?"

Winter nodded. She felt tense and nervous but also excited. Excited that later today, she would be reunited with Autumn— excited to be doing something positive, proactive about her situation.

And weirdly happy that she was wearing a ring on her left hand. It might only be a 'pretend' wedding band, but just the feel of it, just the way Satchel had slid the platinum band onto her ring finger made her feel closer to him. To everyone else in the world, they were married—only she and Satchel knew it was a ruse.

Which might be why Mallory Kline glanced at the ring almost in disbelief. "So... congrats."

"Thank you."

Winter felt nervous around this woman. Mallory was gorgeous, blonde, powerful, uber-confident—and had obviously had the hots for Satchel at one time. Winter wondered if jealousy would play a part in this, but Satchel had assured her that Mallory was a friend.

Still, there was a tension in the air between them. Mallory

nodded, tapping her notebook. "So, Satchel suggested this sit down with you. I have tried to get this story written before, but your sister shut me down. So, to have you here is both a surprise and, I hope, something we can both gain from." Suddenly Mallory grinned. "And, clearly, I needed to check out the competition. What I realize now, Winter, is I was never in the race. Seriously, congratulations. Seeing you and Satch together... yeah, that makes sense."

Winter chuckled with relief, her body relaxing. "Thank, Mallory, I mean it. Can I say I'm glad I wasn't in a competition with you? Because I'd lose."

"Not a chance but thank you anyway." Mallory smiled at her, a genuine friendly smile. "I've only known Satchel a year or so, but I like him immensely. Promise me you'll never hurt him and we're good."

"I promise with all my heart." Winter smiled a little shyly. "And maybe we can be friends? I seem to not have a whole bunch, but those I do, I treasure." She laughed as Mallory offered her a fist bump, and she touched her hand to the other woman's. Mallory had a tomboyishness about her that Winter identified with. "And also, thank you for not pursuing this when my sister asked you not too. Thanks for the respect."

"You're welcome but I have to admit the more I researched, the deeper down the rabbit hole I went. It was a wrench to leave it behind, so when you called, I was surprised."

Winter nodded, her smile fading. "Well, call it facing my demons. The loss of my sister, the estrangement from my family, the shooting—"

"—the relationship with Raziel Ganz."

Winter drew in a deep breath. "Yes. And I'll tell you all about it, Mallory, everything. But in your piece... I'd like you to play it down. Not for any other reason—"

"—than you protecting your reputation?"

"No." Winter fixed the other woman with a steady gaze. "For no other reason than to piss Ganz off."

There was a short silence, then a smile spread across Mallory's face. "You want to make him do something reckless? Humiliate him so he has to come after you?"

Winter nodded. "I need a good reason for him to be made to pay for his actions."

"By using yourself as bait." Mallory's smile faded. "Winter..."

"Before you say anything, just know. I'm not alone in this. The FBI knows about my plan."

Mallory's eyes narrowed. "But Satchel doesn't, does he?"

"No. And it needs to stay that way. There's someone else that needs protecting, and I need Satchel to stay focused."

"Who?"

Winter only hesitated for a second before she replied. "Our daughter."

Mallory's eyebrows shot up. "Your daughter? You and Satchel have a child?"

Winter nodded. "That was the reason I left Portland." She swallowed and went on, smoothly 'explaining' that she and Satchel were lovers when she was 'with' Ganz. "Although there was no *actual* relationship with Mr. Ganz," she lied smoothly. "Regardless of any assertion he might make, Raziel knew clearly that our liaisons were casual. When I met Satchel, I broke things off with Raziel."

Mallory nodded. "Winter, when the fire destroyed your home, when you were in the hospital, the staff there told me that Mr Ganz portrayed himself as your fiancé."

"I was never engaged to Raziel. I don't know why he decided to tell people that. If you speak to the doctor treating me, she'll tell you that I did not want him to continue with that narrative." She was choosing her words carefully now, but she saw the light of understanding in Mallory's eyes.

Mallory studied her for a second and then shut off her voice recorder. "Winter, off the record... do you think Raziel torched your place?"

"Yes," Winter said immediately. "I have absolutely no doubt. I just can't prove it."

Mallory considered and then nodded, switching her recorder back on. "So, you left with Satchel? Where did you go?"

"That," Winter said with a smile, "will be my secret. We had friends who offered me a safe place while I was pregnant, and then Satchel and I welcomed our daughter in August." She was fudging the dates of Sukie's birth by a couple of months.

"Why a safe place? Safe? Did you believe you were at risk?"

"Raziel Ganz is a powerful man. After claiming he was my fiancé at the hospital, I knew he would not be easily left behind. I'm sorry if that sounds hard, but no means no, and I told Raziel *no* many, many times. When he was arrested—and I know the charges were dropped —but I knew I had made the right decision to leave."

"Let's move on to your relationship with your eldest sister. Autumn Mai looked for you, I believe, but you chose to remove yourself entirely from her life. How now do you feel about that decision?"

Winter hesitated. "My family... we have been fractured for a while. Since the St Anne's Massacre. There was a miscommunication and a lot of resentment, a lot of guilt, on both sides. At the time I left Portland, I believed my sister no longer wanted a relationship with me. I was told by Raziel Ganz that Autumn had washed her hands of me, even after the houseboat fire." Her voice shook with sadness and anger. "I believed him. I believed him until I saw my sister on the *Today* show."

"Do you think you will be reconciled?"

Winter smiled. Mallory knew very well that she would see Autumn that afternoon—she had helped arrange it. "I do. Very much."

AFTER THE INTERVIEW, Mallory shoved her recorder and pad into her bag and smiled at Winter. "That is the first part over and done with," she said. "When you've seen Autumn, let me know if she's up for the joint interview."

"I will."

"In the meantime, let's talk about how we can rile Ganz up. He might have had the charges dropped, but he knows he's on thin ice."

Winter nodded. "The thing is about Raziel is that I think he'd burn it all down—no pun intended—just to win one argument. He wants me back. But I don't even believe it's so he can have a romantic relationship with me. I'm a possession, is all. Raz doesn't like other boys playing with his toys. Eww," she laughed suddenly, "that's a gross euphemism but you know what I mean."

Mallory wasn't smiling. "He's a dangerous man, Win."

Winter's smile faded. "I know, and he knows I that do. That's what the meeting with Autumn at the gala was all about—he's giving me an ultimatum."

"And you're going to hand yourself over to him?"

"No. I'm just not hiding. If he comes after me... then we'll make sure he goes down."

Mallory shook her head. "Risky."

"Yes, but I'm not willing to let anyone else pay for my mistake. I entered into a sexual... thing.. with Raziel voluntarily. If he thinks he can 'own' me, he's got another thing coming."

When Mallory had left, Winter called Satchel waiting patiently down in the lobby, and he came up to the room. She went into his arms. "How did it go?" His lips were against her hair.

"Good, I think. I liked her." Winter smiled up at him. "Thanks for respecting my wish to see her on my own."

"I'm not saying not knowing what was going on wasn't driving me mad," he chuckled, and Winter laughed.

"Nothing you didn't already know." God, she hated lying to him. "I told her Sukie was born last August," she said, searching his eyes. "I told her she was yours."

"She is mine in all but DNA. And according to the new birth certificate, she's that, too."

Winter half-smiled. "We're crims."

"We are, but for the best reason. Besides, unless we actually use the fake certificates for any official reason... we're fine. All we need is for Raziel to believe it." He smoothed the hair over her ear. "Good thing is she looks just like her beautiful Momma, and nothing like her father."

Winter relaxed. That was true. Sukie could be Winter's mini-me. Even her eyes were more green than blue, not as vivid as Satchel's, but enough so she could easily pass for his daughter.

She felt Satchel's hands sliding up and down her back and nestled closer to him. "We still have a few hours before Autumn arrives." She drew in a deep breath. "Your friend told her it was to meet a potential investor?"

Satchel nodded. "Asha told her a cover story. Autumn has no idea it's you she's meeting. And... I think I should be AWOL for that meeting, too. I never told you this but when you were in the hospital after the shooting... Autumn and I clashed once. She caught me holding your hand and went crazy. She knew I was Callan's best friend—I think she was afraid I was trying to silence you—God, to have her think that—and she bawled me out." He half-smiled. "I'm surprised that didn't wake you from your coma. Anyway, long story short, I think she still hates me and always will."

"No. Once she gets to know you, to know that you're my best friend, my lover..."

"Don't count on it..." But Winter distracted him by kissing him and tugging him towards the bedroom.

Inside, she stripped off his sweater and T-shirt as his fingers unzipped her dress. They fell onto the bed, naked, and their hands moved all over the other's body. Winter felt at her most free like this, with her love, her heart, and the way their bodies moved together. She hooked her legs around his waist as he thrust into her, urging him deeper and harder.

Satchel kissed her deeply as they made love, and she moaned with ecstasy as he made her come again and again. He buried his face in her neck as he too reached his peak, murmuring her name over and over.

Afterward, they showered together, and Winter dressed for the reunion with her sister. Nerves took over and her fingers shook so badly when she tried to button her dress that Satchel had to gently push them aside and do it himself.

Winter touched his face. "I love you, Satchel Rose."

"As I love you, baby. You ready?"

And with a smile, she nodded.

CHAPTER TWENTY-NINE

Autumn walked into the hotel and asked for her client at the reception desk. She knew she was early, but she wanted to get her head together before she met a potential investor.

Ever since she had arrived in Portland, she had been running around town asking questions, trying to find out what had happened to her sister.

The chance meeting with Raziel Ganz in New York had, as far as Autumn was concerned, at least given her some insight into Winter's life in Portland.

Ganz, a charmer with an edge, had readily admitted he had been in love with Winter. "Sadly, I don't think she felt the same way," he'd said with regret. "But I would at least like to know what happened to her."

Autumn had wondered if Ganz was genuine, but after the benefit, it hadn't taken her long to discover his history and the recent FBI investigation. But he'd hooked her with the knowledge of her sister, and when he learned she would be in Portland, he'd invited her to have dinner with him. At first she'd demurred but wanting to know more about his relationship with Winter, she'd agreed to see him.

First though, her agent, Will, had set up this meeting. As soon as Autumn had found out her sister had made a life in Portland, she had been looking into opening a new restaurant here, so she'd have an excuse to be near Winter—if and when she was found. Even if her plans were at the earliest stages, Will told her she'd need backing in the area.

So, to get through this meeting, she'd had to pull her focus from Winter. Now, as she waited to be called to the meeting room, she sorted through her usual go-to pitch material.

She got absorbed and didn't notice the young receptionist approach her.

"Ms. Mai? They said you can go on up now, and there's no need to knock, go right on in. It's the penthouse suite."

Autumn thanked the young woman and gathered her things, heading toward the elevator. It was eerily quiet in the hotel and in the corridor leading to the penthouse. She took a deep breath in and pushed open the door. There was no one in the lobby so she walked towards the living room.

As she stepped into the room, the sun was shining through the window, low winter sun, and for a second it blinded her. Then someone blocked the light and Autumn gasped. For a moment, she thought it was Summer, that she was hallucinating. The woman in front of her was wearing a dress, her long dark hair hanging past her shoulders and a wary look in her eyes.

Finally, she found her voice. "Winter?"

Her youngest sister, looking so beautiful she could cry, smiled tentatively at her. "Hello Auttie."

Time stopped for a second before the sisters flew into each other's arms and sobbed.

THEY BOTH HAD to calm themselves down, but Autumn clung onto Winter's hand as if she was afraid to let go. The sisters sat together on the couch, arms around the other. For a long time, they stared at each other.

"I'm so sorry, Autumn," Winter said eventually. "I know I've hurt you so badly."

"No, *I'm* sorry. I should have tried to find you before, to try to rebuild our family. Losing Summer was like—"

"—dying." They said it together and Winter nodded. "It killed our family."

"And as horrifying as it was, you know what? Summer would have kicked our asses in her gentle way. I keep hearing the words she would have said; I've said them over and over to myself over the years." Autumn wiped her eyes. "She would have told us to celebrate the fact that you *lived*. That you made it through when no one thought you would."

"I wish it had been Summer. It should have been Summer." Winter was crying now but Autumn hugged her hard.

"Why do you always say that?"

"Because she was the good one! She never argued with anyone or made selfish decisions or..."

"Oh, Winter... none of those things make you a bad person, baby. None. Both Summer and I would have both swapped places with you. Summer wasn't perfect. None of us are. She didn't deserve to die like that but neither did you. Oh, love." Autumn began to cry in earnest as she held her sister.

Winter sobbed out all the pain and heartache, cried for her lost sister, for her aunt, for Autumn who'd been left alone. Eventually, she calmed down as Autumn dug a sheaf of tissues from her purse and helped Winter wipe her eyes as well as her own.

For a while, they just looked at each other, and then, glancing down, Autumn touched Winter's left hand, her mouth forming an 'O' of surprise. "You're married?"

Winter nodded, her eyes growing wary. "Yes."

Autumn studied her. "And you have a child, don't you? I heard him or her when you called... it was you, wasn't it? After my *Today* appearance. When I sobbed all over Hoda?"

Winter laughed at Autumn's grimace. "There will be snot."

"There was... copious amounts. But seriously, boo... you have a kid?"

Winter smiled. "Sukie." Her smile wavered. "She's with her daddy at the moment."

"She's here in Portland? Doh," Autumn smacked her own forehead. "Of course she is... God, Winter, we have so much to catch up on. Can I meet her? And who the hell are you married to?"

Winter took a deep breath. "Auttie..."

"No," Autumn read her mind. "No more secrets, Winter. Whatever, whoever."

Winter stared at her for a long moment, then snagged her phone from her pocket and dialed a number. "Baby? Can you bring Sukie to the suite? Yes, really. It's time Autumn knew everything."

As they waited, Autumn studied her sister. "You seem older. I don't mean that as an insult, but you're quieter... no, not quieter but... God, what am I trying to say? Despite everything, you seem serene. Is it him, your husband?"

Winter nodded but said nothing else. When they heard the door open, Winter got up and went out to see her husband, and Autumn heard them talking in low voices.

She stood as Winter came back in, carrying the most gorgeous child she'd ever seen. "Oh Winnie... she's beautiful."

Winter smiled and handed the baby to her sister. "Say hello to your Auntie Autumn, Sukie Summer."

Autumn took Sukie, cradling her in her arms. Sukie stared up at her with her big green-blue eyes, olive skin, her dark black hair covering her little head. "Sukie Summer?"

Winter nodded. "It suits her don't you think?"

"I do. How old did you say she was?"

Winter told her and Autumn frowned a bit. "She's a big baby."

"She is. Her daddy is tall." Winter turned. "You can come in now.

Autumn looked up, smiling, ready to greet her new brother-in-law, but when he stepped into the light, a shock went through her.

Satchel Rose. She stared at her old enemy. "What the hell is this?"

Winter went to her husband's side and took his hand. "Hello, Autumn," Satchel said carefully. "It's good to see you again."

Autumn looked at her sister. "Is this a joke?"

Winter shook her head, obviously prepared for her shock. "No, Auttie, it's not. I love Satchel. He loves me. We are a family."

So many emotions flooded through her and Autumn closed her eyes, hugging her niece to her tightly. Even the sight of his handsome face brought back the terrible nights at the hospital, waiting to see if Winter would live or die, all the while grieving for Summer. She remembered the night she had caught him sitting with Winter, holding her hand, and she'd screamed all her hurt, all her rage at him.

He was Callan Flint's best friend, for the love of God. "I don't understand." She hadn't realized she had spoken aloud until Winter answered her.

"We met in Portland, by accident. At a party. I threw my drink over him." She and Satchel shared a look then. "We met again and talked." Winter went to Autumn's side. "I knew right then I had been angry at the wrong person. The only person to be angry at is locked away and won't ever be released, Autumn. Satchel lost his best friend, too."

Autumn glared at Satchel. "You testified on his behalf."

"I just told the truth as I knew it," Satchel said gently. "There were no signs, nothing to indicate Callan would do what he did. Autumn, I'm so sorry. If I could bring Summer back, I would in a heartbeat."

"But you can't." She flicked her eyes to Winter. "So you decided to knock up my sister and salve your guilt that way?"

"Auttie, stop. We fell in love."

Autumn felt both sad and angry. "And you couldn't find someone better than a psycho's best friend? A creep who took to holding your hand while you were in a coma, for Chrissakes?"

"That's enough." Winter's face flushed with anger. "Satchel is not a creep. He is the man I love, and God, Auttie, if you only knew what he has done to save my life, to protect Sukie."

Autumn felt a jolt. "Why would he need to protect Sukie?"

Winter's face turned even redder, and she looked away from her sister's penetrating gaze. Suddenly Autumn knew. "Oh, my God. She's not your daughter, is she? She's Raziel Ganz's child…"

"No…"

"Yes." Satchel interrupted Winter, nodding at Autumn. "She's his biological child. But Sukie is my daughter, just as Winter is my wife. Raziel Ganz is a criminal and a psychopath. Yes, a psycho, just like Callan. We removed Winter and Sukie from Portland to protect them."

"So, why are you back now?" Autumn's emotions were in a turmoil.

"Because I'm sick of hiding." Winter spoke finally. "Raziel… I can't prove it, but I know in my bones he set that fire on my houseboat. He set it so he could 'save' me, so I'd be forever grateful to him. I'd broken things off with him because he got possessive and violent." Winter held her hands out for her daughter, and Autumn reluctantly gave her up.

"Auttie, I was pregnant when the fire happened. Only a few weeks but I didn't have it confirmed until the hospital. Ganz doesn't know Sukie exists."

Autumn's jaw clenched. "He doesn't know?"

"The man is a human trafficker and a criminal," Satchel said. "If he'd found them…"

Autumn felt sick. She had known Ganz was a player, but could she really believe everything they were telling her? Satchel Rose… he seemed genuine, but what if he were the man behind the curtain? He always seemed to be involved when bad things happened—his best friend, Callan—maybe Satchel had in fact known about his plans and egged him on? The way he was looking at Winter now… could it be he was the possessive, obsessive one?

God, she was so mixed up. "I have to get out of here."

Winter's face creased with distress. "No, Autumn, please don't go."

But Autumn was already halfway out of the door. "I need to think, Win." She stopped as she reached the door and turned to look at her sister. "Don't disappear again. Please. I just need to think."

Winter nodded, her eyes filling with tears. Autumn had to force herself not to go to her. Instead she looked at Sukie, so peaceful in her mother's arms. "She really is a beautiful baby."

And, choking back a sob, she fled.

CHAPTER THIRTY

Winter stood frozen, starting slightly when Satchel slid his arms around her, kissing her temple. "It's going to be okay, baby."

She nodded, leaning into him. "I thought she might react like this." She gave him a weary half-smile. "But at least she didn't throw her drink on you."

"I'm more concerned about her connection to Ganz."

Winter blinked. "What?"

"She's meeting him tonight."

Winter stepped away from him and turned to face him. "Satchel... are you having my sister followed?"

Satchel looked unrepentant. "Yes. Ever since she met with Ganz at the benefit. For her protection, for yours, for Sukie's. I don't trust his motives."

Winter felt a little sick, and he touched her face. "Baby, I swear, I'm not trying to invade everyone's privacy. It's just... this time..."

Suddenly Winter got it. "Oh God... this is in reaction to Callan again, isn't it?"

"Of course it is!" Satchel's outburst made Sukie wake, and she wailed. Winter rocked her, calming her. "I'm sorry," Satchel said, holding his hands up. "But *of course* it is. I couldn't protect you last time, but God knows, I'm going to do everything in my power to protect you all this time."

Sukie wouldn't settle. Winter nodded and moved to the bedroom. "I'll feed her and put her down for a nap."

Satchel sighed. "I'll go get us some takeout."

"We could just get room service."

He shook his head. "No, I need some air. Chinese, okay?"

Winter nodded, searching his face. Was he mad at her? "Okay, baby. I love you."

His face softened. "And I love you, darling. I won't be long."

WINTER FED SUKIE and put her down to sleep. She checked the living room, but Satchel wasn't back yet. She risked a call to Guy Holbrook. The FBI agent greeted her warmly. "How's our plan coming along?"

"Well, I met with Mallory Kline and set the ball rolling. She told me she was going to release a teaser of the interview loaded with a jibe at Raziel. We'll see how he reacts."

Guy Holbrook sighed. "I still think baiting him is too risky."

"As long as Satchel, Autumn, and my daughter are protected, it's a risk worth taking."

"You should at least clue Satchel in to our endgame."

Winter rubbed her face. "Agent Holbrook, if Raziel kills me... you'll have no reason to tell Satchel you were involved, and you would have gotten your reason to put him away forever."

"What about you?"

"I got involved with Raziel voluntarily. This is my mess to clear up."

"Jesus." She heard Holbrook sighed. "I hate this; I hate putting you at risk. Seriously, Winter, why put yourself through this? Why come back from New Orleans? What do you get out of this, really?"

Winter swallowed hard before she answered. "Freedom. One way or the other."

. . .

RAZIEL WALKED INTO HIS STATEROOM, ready to change for his dinner with Autumn Mai, when his cell phone buzzed. It was one of his team. "Hey, boss."

"What you got for me?"

"Winter Mai is in Portland."

That stopped Raz in his tracks. "She's here?" Incredulous, Raz sat down. Winter was back in Portland? "How do you know?"

"We were following her sister, and she met Winter at a hotel in the city. Boss, Winter was with Satchel Rose. We paid off a staff member. They're together. Married. And, boss, they have a kid."

What the actual fuck? "A child?"

"A baby. Our contact thinks almost six months."

Shock and Anger flooded Raziel's system. "That fucking little *bitch*."

"What do you want us to do, boss?"

Raziel was silent for a moment. "Nothing. Leave it with me. Just keep surveillance on them. All of them but keep your distance. I'll decide what to do in a little while."

HE SAT on the bed after he ended the call, seething. Now he had no doubt that Winter had left Portland because she had been pregnant, and that meant that she'd been sleeping with Satchel Rose back then... or the kid was his own. *Fucking bitch.* If she was here right now, he would clamp his hands around her throat and squeeze until she was blue...

Raziel took some deep breaths. *Don't lose control now.* Tonight, he would see Autumn and try to get a read on the situation, on her reunion with her sister. Why was Winter back in Portland? She knew what would happen if Raziel caught up with her...

Unless...

Winter wanted him to come for her. He smiled grimly. *That's a rookie movie, Winter.* Entrapment? He shook his head. He couldn't believe Rose—God, her husband—had agreed to this, knowing what he did. They were trying to goad him into acting—the message was clear. Come for Winter and the FBI will have all the evidence they need to put you away for life.

No. He'd have to be more careful. Use people who couldn't be traced back to him. One thing he did know was that Winter and Rose would be made to pay for their betrayal. *There's no happy ever after for you, my beautiful Winter...*

Smiling grimly, Raziel got up to change for dinner.

AUTUMN STOOD in the shower longer than she intended, letting the hot water flood down her body, easing the tension in her tight shoulders. Her mind raced with everything she'd learned today. Winter was married to Satchel Rose and had a daughter by Raziel Ganz who she was publicly naming as Satchel's.

Satchel Rose. God, she had hated that man for years, ever since she had sat through his testimony in defense of the man who murdered her sister. She still remembered his time on the witness stand...

There were no signs... he was my best friend... I loved him...

The sadness in those beautiful green eyes, the torment. He had looked shattered. Autumn remembered him sobbing as he recalled finding out that Callan had been responsible for the massacre... *It doesn't make any sense, it doesn't make any sense...*

At the time, her anger and grief had made her cynical, her twisted emotions telling her that it was a rich boy protecting another rich boy.

When she'd seen him at the hospital with a comatose Winter she had had flipped out, screaming at him to get the hell away from her sister, that he'd done enough to destroy their family...

But now, she had to admit, that he wasn't the monster she's built up in her head. Seeing him tonight, obviously so in love with Winter and Sukie, the child of another man... Satchel Rose wasn't who she'd thought he was.

And that was what was messing with her head. Was her perception of the world so fucked up?

Yes. "Shut up," she told herself and stepped out of the shower, cranking the water off. She tugged a dress from the suitcase, not caring which one—she wasn't going to get too gussied up for Raziel Ganz. *Huh,* she thought, Winter's opinion of the man, her terror that he would discover the existence of Sukie... Autumn wondered if she should cancel the dinner, but there was something in her that was curious to know more about the man. Was he really as corrupt, as dangerous as they said? She wanted to push his buttons, see the real man beneath the smooth exterior. If her sister needed protecting from Ganz then by God, Autumn wanted to know everything about him.

As she got into the cab, she went over what Winter had told her. The charges against Ganz had been dropped, but Winter was convinced he was who the FBI told them he was. Bastard. *Well, try anything on me, Ganz, and it'll go public real quick.*

As she arrived at his hotel, she wondered why, if he'd been here in Portland for over a year, he hadn't acquired a permanent home here. *Ready for a quick getaway, Mr Ganz?* Autumn smiled grimly to herself and went inside.

RAZIEL, standing at the window, saw Autumn's cab arrive and the front desk called up to him. "Send Ms. Mai up. We'll have dinner here in the suite."

Not that she'd be staying to eat after what he had to say. He'd decided to play the grieving ex-boyfriend card, the ex-boyfriend who'd found out the love of his life was married and had a child with someone he had considered a friend.

Heartbroken. To all appearances, he would seem to have thrown in the towel, left Portland to return to New York. In reality, he had already set the wheels in motion.

Winter and Satchel would soon learn that nobody cuckolded Raziel Ganz.

CHAPTER THIRTY-ONE

 week later...

"I DON'T BELIEVE THIS."

Winter shook her head at Satchel. "I just don't believe it. Nothing? He's done nothing?"

Mallory Kline's interview had been released onto the internet, and it was even more mocking of Ganz than Winter had intended. Mallory had really come through for them. But Ganz had no reaction: no rebuttal, no denial. He'd just packed up his whole operation in Portland and moved back to New York. Raziel Ganz was gone.

Satchel looked as skeptical as Winter felt. "Yes, I'm not trusting this at all. So, I'm upping the security around you and Sukie. Autumn, too, if she'll let me."

Winter half-smiled. "I think she's warming up to you."

"Hah. We'll see."

They were driving out to Satchel's pet project: his house out on the coast. Worrying about Raziel's reaction to the news of their 'marriage' didn't stop them from making plans for their future, and when Satchel had asked Winter where she wanted to live, she told him that Portland was in her heart.

Satchel had been delighted. Just yesterday, he had taken Winter and Sukie to meet his father and Janelle, and despite the older Roses' doubts early on, they had adored Winter and doted on Sukie. He and Winter had decided to tell them the truth about Sukie's parentage, and Satchel was relieved when his father approved. "Usually I couldn't support denying the father his natural right, but in this case..."

Patrick had kissed Winter's cheek. "Welcome to the family, dear one."

Winter had been overwhelmed by the love they had shown her and even now, as they drove to the new house, she chatted about how much his parents had loved Sukie and made her feel like one of them.

"You are one of us, darling. And, now, I'm going to marry the heck out of you as soon as possible."

Winter giggled at his smug face. "You better ask properly first, dude."

"Oh, I will, I—"

He didn't get to finish that sentence as their car was slammed hard from the side. Winter screamed as it rolled over and over, and as she, Satchel, and a howling Sukie were thrown like rag dolls inside the car.

Winter lost consciousness even before the car stopped rolling.

RAZIEL SMILED as he ended the call. Back in his apartment in Manhattan—finally—he made sure his dinner guests saw his wide smile. "Well, looks like the final charges are about to be dropped."

There was a murmuring as he raised his glass. "I want to thank you all for the support you have shown me during this farcical court case. To say that I, of all people, could be involved with something so..." He cast around for the right word. "... so disgusting, so vile as human trafficking? Christ..." He shook his head in exaggerated disgust. A good few of the people in this room knew *exactly* what he did for a living but were too afraid of him to say otherwise. Most, though, remained in blissful ignorance. They raised their glasses to him, beaming their relief at him. An angry cornered Raziel was nothing they wanted anything to do with.

The few friends who had shunned him now would soon find their businesses failing and their wives suddenly absent from their marriage beds. Only this afternoon he had fucked the beautiful wife of the main culprit, screwed her so hard she could barely walk. He made sure she went back to her husband reeking of Raziel and sex.

He'd planned on making Autumn Mai his lover, but she had declined to take his calls since that one night at the hotel in Portland. That night, she'd listened to his tale of heartbreak and abandonment by Winter.

"And now, I hear she has married and has a child."

He'd noticed that Autumn had flinched somewhat, but quickly smoothed her expression out. "It's probably time you moved on, Mr. Ganz."

"Raziel, please."

"Raziel." Autumn had tried to smile. "I know it must hurt, but Winter tells me that you and she, well... Both of you knew it was only a casual thing."

She was challenging him to lie—he smiled at her coolly. "For her, perhaps."

"I believe she told you the same thing, several times."

"It's only right that you support your only sister."

Autumn's face paled, and he knew his barb had hit home. Good. "What I mean is, Winter is entitled to believe what she believes, but I saw it differently."

He got up to pour them both drinks. "But perhaps you are right. One cannot force, nor expect, another person to feel the same way one does. For my part, Winter will always be the one who got away."

Autumn's eyes narrowed, and he could see she wasn't buying his innocent act. Raziel was briefly tempted to ask Autumn how she would feel when Winter was dead, too, just to see her reaction. Don't blow it now just for amusement's sake. "Anyway, I hope she and Rose are happy. And they have a daughter, you say?"

He watched as two bright pink spots appeared on Autumn's cheeks, and in that second, he *knew*. Sitting down, casually crossing his legs, he brushed some imaginary dirt of his pants. "The child... a girl?"

Autumn nodded. "Sukie." She looked like she hated even saying the name aloud as if it were some kind of betrayal. Raziel tamped down his anger. *My daughter. My child.* He knew it in his marrow.

"Well, I hope they're happy."

Autumn hadn't stayed much longer and since then it had been radio silence. No matter. He'd known from that second meeting that she would be no more use to him, and the likelihood of getting her into bed, just to spite Winter, was a nonstarter. Autumn Mai was no fool.

Now, as the dinner party broke up, Gareth came to find him. "The plane is ready, Raz. Whenever you are."

Raziel smiled. "My stuff is packed; can you tell the driver I'll be down in a few moments?"

"Sure thing, boss."

Alone at last, he glanced around the apartment. For all the months that he'd been away from this place, tonight would be the very last time he would be here. In this apartment, in this city. In this country. Tonight, he would fly in his private jet down to Rio and he wouldn't be alone.

Because on another plane, flying from a city across the other side of the country, would be a nanny and a wet nurse, bringing his daughter to him.

Water. She was surrounded by water, and it was pouring into her mouth and ears and eyes and it was dark, so dark. She felt someone's arms around her pulling her up, up to where moonlight shone down. *Sukie... Satchel...*

As her head broke the surface of the water, Winter gasped,

choking as Satchel pulled her onto the sand. "Winter! Winter, breathe, honey! Cough the water up!"

He was pounding on her back, and she coughed up ocean water, salty and rank, but all she could think of was her daughter. With her first breath, she gasped out Sukie's name.

"Baby, baby, breathe, calm."

Don't tell me to calm down! Where is my daughter?

"Winter, you have to calm down or the water in your lungs..."

She threw up copious amounts of water and felt Satchel rubbing her back. As she drew in a desperate breath, she gasped Sukie's name again and again, trying to make him understand that was all she cared about.

Her vision blurred and then focused as she looked around to see Satchel, drenched, pale, blood dripping from a nasty head wound as he shook his head, his eyes wild and panicked.

"Where is she?" Winter gasped as terror shot through her, and Satchel could only sob out the answer.

"She's gone... baby. I'm sorry, Sukie's gone."

CHAPTER THIRTY-TWO

W inter stared hollow-eyed and exhausted as the doctor checked her out. Satchel's wounds were so much worse than hers, and he'd been taken into surgery. Two hours. Her daughter had been gone two hours.

She had screamed when Satchel had said the words, but he'd held his hands up immediately. "No, I mean... she's not dead, she's *gone*." The seat belt on Sukie's car seat had been cut. Her daughter had been abducted.

Frantic phone calls to Guy Holbrook. "We're on it, Winter. We'll get her back."

"It's him."

"I know."

And now Winter was calm. Icy calm. An FBI agent from the local Portland office had arrived at the hospital. "We think your car was hit, but it didn't immediately go into the water. Your daughter was cut out of it first, then the car was pushed into the water by the other vehicle."

Winter looked at him. "What now?"

"We've stopped all flights from the surrounding airports, and we're checking every highway and interstate. We'll find her, Winter."

But Winter's rage, anger, and terror meant that was not satisfying. She demanded to speak directly to Holbrook, and when she was put through, she outlined her plan.

"I can't let you do that, Winter."

"Sukie is my daughter, Agent Holbrook. Ever tried to stop a mother protecting her child? Find her."

SATCHEL WAS OPERATED on successfully and as he lay unconscious in his room, Winter bent over and kissed his forehead. She stroked his dark curls away from his forehead. "My love," she whispered, "my one true love. If I don't come back... just know I never regretted one moment I spent with you. But Sukie is my flesh and blood and I have to *try*. I love you so, so much."

Tears poured down her face as she drank him in. The doctors had told her Satchel would be okay, but she knew when he woke, he would be angry about what she had to do. She put the letter she had written to him on the nightstand, and with one last look, she left the room.

Slipping silently down the staircase at the end of the corridor, she nodded to the FBI agent who was waiting outside for her.

RAZIEL STEPPED out into the humid Rio de Janeiro evening and smiled. He got into the waiting cab and stared out of the window as it sped through the night to the little private airport outside the city. It had all gone to plan. Hopefully... Well, he *wished* that Winter had survived the accident and knew now she had lost. His daughter was on her way to him.

He had a lab set up to test the child's DNA—if it turned out Rose was the father...

Raziel winced a little. He'd cross that particular bridge when he came to it.

At the airport, he saw the little plane fly in and land a few feet away from his car. He nodded as he saw Davide carrying a small bundle down the steps of the plane, then frowned. Why was Davide carrying the baby and not the wet nurse or the nanny?

Raziel stepped closer to the bodyguard as Davide approached. There was no smile, no warmth in Davide's eyes, and Raz quickly realized he held nothing in his arms except a bundle of rags.

"What the fuck?"

Davide regarded him calmly. "I don't hold with the kidnapping of children. I've closed my eyes long enough to your evil, Ganz. No more."

Raziel's anger flared. "You piece of shit, where is my daughter?"

"Right here."

Davide stepped aside, and Raziel saw Winter holding Sukie in her arms and standing just a few feet from the plane. Raz shot Davide a glare and stalked over to her. Winter stood her ground.

"You fucking little whore. You kept her from me."

Winter didn't back down. "And I'm going to keep her from you for the rest of your life. She won't even know your name, Raziel. As far as Sukie is concerned, Satchel is her father."

Raziel lunged for her, but Winter sidestepped him and behind her, two FBI agents were waiting to take Raziel down. Raziel raged in their grip. "You have no jurisdiction here!"

One of the agents smiled grimly. "Maybe not. But we're getting back on that plane right there and flying out into international waters. It'll take five minutes to arrest you, Ganz, and this time you won't get away with anything."

Raziel fought with the agents holding him and for a moment, he was able to break free. From his waistband, he brought out a pistol and levelled it at Winter. "You don't get to see her grow up, bitch."

And shots rang out...

CHAPTER THIRTY-THREE

S atchel opened his eyes, his head screaming with pain. He sat up despite the agony and tried to get out of bed. Winter... Where was Winter?

A nurse came in then and gasped. "No, you don't."

In his weakened state, Satchel was no match for the strong woman as she steered him back into bed. "Please," he said, "My wife, my Winter... where is she?"

"I'm right here, baby."

Winter stepped into the room, and in her arms, Sukie was sleeping peacefully. Satchel's whole body slumped in relief. "Sukie..."

"She's fine. I'm fine." Winter smiled at the nurse and thanked her as she left them alone, then she sat on the edge of Satchel's bed. She touched his face. "We were worried about you. You were out longer than the doctor's thought you would be."

"How long?"

"Three days." She looked down at her sleeping daughter. "Sukie was wondering when her daddy would wake up."

Satchel kissed her, then pressed his lips to the sleeping child's forehead. "How... I mean... how did you find her?"

"With a lot, and I mean a *lot*, of help from the FBI. Raziel had her flown to Rio. What he didn't know was I was with her the whole time."

"What? What happened?" Satchel's face hung slack with confusion.

Winter half-smiled. "He's rotting in a Rio prison, awaiting trial for attempted murder. He tried to kill me, of course. He failed."

Satchel shook his head, studying her. "You went to Rio when you could have just brought her back here?"

"Yes." She returned his gaze steadily.

"You knew he would try to kill you?"

"Yes."

Satchel rubbed his pale face. "*Jesus*, Winter."

"I've been working with Guy Holbrook for weeks trying to set up a confrontation. It was the only way he was going to lose control enough for us to get the evidence we need. Now, don't go blaming Holbrook—"

"—you could have been killed!"

"Yes."

Satchel gaped at her. "You are the most reckless, the most... Jesus, Winter..." He looked down at Sukie in her arms. "Wait, you took her with you?"

"There wasn't any time to lose and Sukie needed feeding. But I should have left her on the plane when I confronted him except..."

"Except what?"

Winter looked a little guilty. "I wanted him to see what he had lost. If he hadn't been so... He could have had a relationship with her, but he chose instead to abduct her. So, I wanted him to see what he had lost. Actually," she grimaced ruefully, "I probably wasn't thinking straight at all—I was so angry. Docs think I may have a little concussion. But, seriously, Holbrook sent me backup. They handled it."

"But Raziel tried to kill you."

"He pulled a gun on me—and Davide shot him."

"Davide? His bodyguard?"

"Yup. Davide turned on him. They'll have all the evidence they need now to put Raziel away for good. I'm putting in a word for Davide. Hopefully they'll go lenient on him in court. He saved us."

Satchel sat back against the pillows, his mind whirling. "Thank God." He sighed. "But fuck this head injury, I should have been with you. I failed to save you again."

"What the hell are you talking about? You pulled me from the ocean! You saved me from drowning! Raziel would be in Brazil with our daughter if it wasn't for you! God, Satch..." Winter's calm demeanor collapsed then, and she began to cry softly.

Sukie, awoken by her mother's trembling body, put her little hand up to Winter's face. Satchel wrapped his arms around the both of them. "It's okay, Winter, it's okay... it's all over now..."

She nodded, leaning her head on his shoulder. "We're a family."

"You're my darling wife."

She shook her head, half-laughing. "No, don't call me that anymore. We don't need to pretend anymore. I want to be your wife, Satchel, but I don't want to be called your wife until I actually am. Am I making any sense?"

Satchel smiled at her. "In that case..." He kissed her then Sukie's head. "Winter Mai... it might be a while before I can go down on one knee, but who cares about doing things the traditional way?"

"Not us."

"Not us," he agreed and grinned. "So, Winter Mai... would you do me the extraordinary honor of taking me as your husband?"

Winter's tears flowed unabated, but her smile was radiant. "You bet your sweet little ass I will."

Satchel laughed, and they held each other, talking long into the night, their daughter peaceful in their arms.

CHAPTER THIRTY-FOUR

T wenty-three months later...
    Portland, Oregon

WINTER CLASPED Satchel's hand as the verdicts were read out. *Guilty.*
Guilty. Guilty. It went on and on.

Raziel Ganz stood at the defense table, his expression blank, his
eyes never leaving the foreperson's face as she read out every guilty
verdict. Winter shivered involuntarily; how the hell had she ever let
that man touch her? He exuded evil and malice.

The judge didn't waste time postponing sentencing. Raziel Ganz
was going away for the rest of his life. His allies had either scattered
or been caught or killed by the massive operation that followed his
arrest.

As Raziel was led away, he turned and stared at Winter, his eyes
cold and dead. Winter didn't look away. This was the biological father
of her daughter, the one good thing to come out of the mess she'd
gotten herself into with him. His lawyer had advised him to sign over

all rights to Sukie to Winter in exchange for a more lenient charge, but in the end, it hadn't helped his cause.

For giving up his rights to Sukie, Winter was grateful, but she was glad she would never have to lay eyes on Raziel Ganz ever again. That Sukie, nearly two and a half now and gorgeously entertaining and loud, would never have to know that her biological father would have killed her mommy just because Winter refused to be 'with' him. She was determined her daughter would be brought up knowing her own worth and that she had her own agency in every relationship in her life.

And that she had a daddy who loved her. As soon as Raziel signed over his rights, Satchel had begun the process of adopting Sukie, helped by his ex-girlfriend, the family lawyer, Asha, to whom Winter had grown very close. Only three days ago the final ruling had come through, and now Sukie Mai was Sukie Summer Rose, sharing a surname with both her mommy and her new daddy.

Satchel and Winter had married a few months after Satchel proposed after he completely recovered from his injuries, and they had spent time as a family together. The wedding, held at his father's place, was followed by an Italian honeymoon with their daughter.

Now, as they walked out of the courthouse, they were surrounded by journalists. Satchel only took questions from one—Mallory. She grinned at them both. "How are you doing, kiddos?"

Satchel grinned, and they bore Mallory off to the restaurant where they were meeting their family and friends. As they celebrated the final chapter in the case, Satchel and Winter took a quiet moment to themselves as their loved ones drank champagne.

Satchel took Winter's hand and led her to a quiet corner of the restaurant. He pressed his lips to hers and she smiled up at him. "It's really over."

"It is, my love."

They held each other for a long time until they heard Janelle call out for them, and they joined hands and walked back to their party.

. . .

JANELLE BORE Sukie off to stay the night with her and Patrick, and Satchel drove himself and Winter home to their oceanside home. They had moved into it soon after Winter and Sukie returned from Rio, and it was their haven.

Now, as they stepped inside, Winter sighed with relief and happiness. Satchel grinned at her and drew her close. "So... we have the house to ourselves..."

She giggled. "Oh, and I wonder what we could do?"

Satchel pressed his lips to her neck. "Wifey?"

"Hubby?" Winter closed her eyes as he trailed his lips along her jaw. She shivered with pleasure as his lips met hers.

Satchel picked her up, and she wrapped her legs around his waist as he carried her to the bedroom. Winter laughed as he dumped her unceremoniously on the bed, and grinning widely, jumped on top of her. "Oh, you silly, silly man..."

He pretended to bite down on her neck as she giggled, then they were tearing each other's clothes off, kissing, tickling each other, and laughing.

When they were naked, Satchel gently drew her legs around his hips and thrust into her. He gazed down at her as they moved together, his hands cradling her face. "God, I love you, Winter Rose."

Winter smiled up at him. "As I love you. Everything from now on is just going to be joy, isn't it?"

"You bet your gorgeous little butt it is." They both laughed, but then the intensity of their lovemaking grew, and they stopped talking and continued loving long into the night...

THE END

ABOUT THE AUTHOR

Mrs. Love writes about smart, sexy women and the hot alpha billionaires who love them. She has found her own happily ever after with her dream husband and adorable 6 and 2 year old kids. Currently, Michelle is hard at work on the next book in the series, and trying to stay off the Internet.

"Thank you for supporting an indie author. Anything you can do, whether it be writing a review, or even simply telling a fellow reader that you enjoyed this. Thanks

❀ Created with Vellum

CPSIA information can be obtained
at www.ICGtesting.com
Printed in the USA
BVHW040757060121
597036BV00012B/56